BY JANET EVANOVICH

THE FOX AND O'HARE NOVELS WITH LEE GOLDBERG

The Heist   *The Job*
The Chase

THE STEPHANIE PLUM NOVELS

One for the Money   *Twelve Sharp*
Two for the Dough   *Lean Mean Thirteen*
Three to Get Deadly   *Fearless Fourteen*
Four to Score   *Finger Lickin' Fifteen*
High Five   *Sizzling Sixteen*
Hot Six   *Smokin' Seventeen*
Seven Up   *Explosive Eighteen*
Hard Eight   *Notorious Nineteen*
To the Nines   *Takedown Twenty*
Ten Big Ones   *Top Secret Twenty-One*
Eleven on Top

THE BETWEEN THE NUMBERS STORIES

Visions of Sugar Plums   *Plum Lucky*
Plum Lovin'   *Plum Spooky*

THE LIZZY AND DIESEL NOVELS

Wicked Appetite   *Wicked Business*

THE ALEXANDRA BARNABY NOVELS

Metro Girl   *Troublemaker* (graphic novel)
Motor Mouth

NONFICTION

How I Write

THE JOB

THE JOB

A FOX AND O'HARE NOVEL

JANET EVANOVICH
AND LEE GOLDBERG

BANTAM BOOKS NEW YORK

Copyright © 2014 by The Gus Group LLC

Published in the United States by Bantam Books, an imprint of Random House, a division of Random House LLC, a Penguin Random House Company, New York.

BANTAM BOOKS and the HOUSE colophon are registered trademarks of Random House LLC.

LIBRARY OF CONGRESS CATALOGING-IN-PUBLICATION DATA
Evanovich, Janet.
The job: a Fox and O'Hare novel / Janet Evanovich and Lee Goldberg.
pages; cm.—(Fox and O'Hare; 3)
ISBN 978-0-345-54312-7
eBook ISBN 978-0-345-54314-1
1. United States. Federal Bureau of Investigation—Fiction. 2. Government investigators—Fiction. 3. Women detectives—Fiction. 4. Swindlers and swindling—Fiction. I. Goldberg, Lee, 1962– II. Title.
PS3555.V2126J66 2014813'.54—dc23 2014035375

Printed in the United States of America on acid-free paper

www.bantamdell.com

2   4   6   8   9   7   5   3   1

First Edition

Book design by Liz Cosgrove

ACKNOWLEDGMENTS

We'd like to thank Craig Barron, James T. Clemente, Serge Dintroz, Dallas Murphy, Mark Safarik, and Jenny White for sharing their knowledge and experience with us. We hope they won't mind the creative liberties we've taken and will forgive us for any mistakes we've made.

THE JOB

1

FBI Special Agent Kate O'Hare slouched back in her tan leather executive office chair, looked across her desk, and surveyed the lobby of the Tarzana branch of California Metro Bank. The desk actually belonged to the assistant manager. Kate was occupying it because she was waiting for the bank to get robbed. She'd been waiting four days, and she was wishing it would happen soon, because she was going gonzo with boredom.

The boredom vanished and her posture improved when two businessmen wearing impeccably tailored suits walked through the bank's double glass doors. One of the men wore Ray-Bans and had a Louis Vuitton backpack slung over his shoulder. The other man was stylishly unshaven and had a raincoat draped casually over his right arm. It hadn't rained in L.A. in two months, and no rain was expected, so Kate figured these might be the guys she'd been waiting to arrest, and that one of them wasn't all that good at hiding a weapon.

The man wearing the Ray-Bans went directly into the manager's glass-walled office. The man with the raincoat approached Kate's desk and sat down across from her. His gaze immediately went to her chest, which was entirely understandable, as she was wearing a push-up bra under her Ann Taylor pantsuit that made her breasts burst out of her open blouse like Poppin' Fresh dough. This wasn't a favored look for Kate, but she was *the job,* and if it took cleavage to capture some slimeball, then she was all about it.

"May I help you, sir?" Kate asked.

"Call me Slick," the man said.

"Slick?" she said. "Really?"

He shrugged and adjusted the raincoat so that she could see the Sig Sauer 9mm semiautomatic underneath it. "Keep smiling and relax. I'm simply a businessman talking to you about opening a new account."

Kate glanced toward the office of the manager. FBI Special Agent Seth Ryerson was behind the manager's desk, and the real manager was working as one of the bank's four tellers. The Ray-Bans guy was giving Ryerson instructions. Ryerson turned to look at Kate, and she could see that sweat was already beading on his balding head. As soon as any action started, Ryerson always broke out in a sweat. In five minutes, he'd be soaked. It was never pretty.

Kate and Ryerson had been working undercover, following

a tip, hoping the men would show up. The bank fit the profile of the six other San Fernando Valley banks the Businessman Bandits had held up over the last two months. The Tarzana bank was a stand-alone building in a largely residential area and was within a block of a freeway on-ramp and a major interchange.

Kate knew there was a third "businessman" in a car idling in the parking lot. She also knew that an FBI strike team was parked around the corner waiting to move in.

"What do you want me to do?" Kate asked Slick.

"Sit there and be pretty. Here's how it's going to work, sweetie. My associate is telling your manager to take the backpack to the vault and bring it back filled with cash or I will put a bullet in your chest. My associate will then leave the bank, but I will stick around for a minute flirting with you. If any dye packs explode, or any alarms go off, I will shoot you. If nothing goes wrong, I'll simply get up and walk out the door, no harm done. All you have to do is stay calm, and this will all be over soon."

It was the same speech he'd given to the women at the other banks the Businessman Bandits had held up. Slick always picked a young woman with cleavage to threaten with his gun, which was why Kate had worn the push-up bra. She'd wanted to be his target.

Kate looked past Slick to the lobby and the bank tellers. There were seven customers in the bank, four at the counter and three in line. No one seemed to notice that anything unusual was happening. Ryerson left the Ray-Bans guy in his office and took the Vuitton backpack to the vault.

Kate's iPhone vibrated on her desk. JAMES BOND showed up on the caller ID.

"Ignore it," Slick said. "Look at me instead."

Kate shifted her gaze back to Slick's carefully unshaven face, his stubble a shadow on his thin cheeks and sharp chin. The phone went still. After fifteen seconds it began to vibrate again. James Bond wasn't a man who gave up easily.

"That's annoying," Slick said. "Do you always take personal phone calls during work hours?"

"If they're important."

The phone continued to vibrate.

"Shut it off," Slick said. *"Now."*

Kate shut the phone down. A moment later her desk phone rang.

"I don't like this," Slick said. "On your feet. We're walking out of here."

"It's just a phone call," Kate said. "It's probably my mother."

"Up!" he said. "And start walking. If anyone approaches you, I'm shooting you first and then whoever else gets in my way. Clear?"

This isn't good, Kate thought. There were customers conducting business, coming and going, and there was a possibility that one of them would accidentally cross their path.

"Should I take my purse?"

"No."

"Won't it look odd if I walk out of the bank without my purse?"

"Where is it?"

"The bottom drawer, to my right."

"Stay where you are, and I'll open the drawer. Do *not* move."

He stood and moved around the desk, all the while keeping his eyes on Kate. He held the Sig in his right hand and reached down to open the drawer with his left. The instant his attention shifted from Kate to the drawer, she smacked him hard in the face with her keyboard. His eyes went blank, the gun dropped from his hand, blood gushed out of his smashed nose, and he crashed to the floor, unconscious.

Kate picked the gun up and aimed it at his partner in the manager's office.

"FBI!" she yelled. "Don't move. Put your hands on your head."

Mr. Ray-Bans did as he was told. Everyone in the bank froze, too, startled by her outburst and shocked by the sight of her holding the gun.

Ryerson rushed out of the vault, his gun drawn, big sweat stains under his armpits. He looked confused. "What happened?"

"I had to go to Plan B," Kate said. She turned to the customers in the bank. "Relax, everyone. We have the situation entirely under control, and you aren't in any danger."

Kate's desk phone wouldn't stop ringing. She kept her gun aimed at Mr. Ray-Bans in the manager's office, and snatched at the phone with her other hand.

"What?" she said.

"Is that any way to talk to James Bond?"

"You're not James Bond."

It was Nick Fox, and truth is, Kate thought Nick was pretty darn close to James Bond. A little younger and mostly on the other side of the law, but just as lethal and just as sexy.

Fox was a world-class con man and thief. Kate had tracked him for years and finally captured him, only to have her boss, Carl Jessup, and Fletcher Bolton, the deputy director of the FBI, arrange Nick's escape. In return for conditional freedom, Nick had agreed to use his unique skills to nail big-time criminals the Bureau couldn't catch using conventional means.

Kate had been given the unwanted responsibility of helping Nick neutralize the bad guys. She was also supposed to make sure Nick didn't go back to his life of crime. The Bureau didn't have Nick under constant surveillance or wearing a tracking device between assignments, so it was up to Kate to keep him on a loose leash. It had been a few days since she'd last spoken to him.

"Did I catch you at a bad time?" Nick asked.

"Yes. What do you want?"

"I didn't do it."

Kate went silent for a beat. She had no clue what he was talking about, but whatever it was, at least he hadn't done it. That was good, right?

"I'm kind of busy right now," she said.

"No problem. I just thought you'd want to know."

Kate hung up, and the phone rang again. It was Carl Jessup.

"Your cellphone isn't working," Jessup said.

"That's because I'm in the middle of a bank robbery thing."

"We've got a big problem," Jessup said in his distinctive Kentucky twang. "Yesterday, Nicolas Fox stole a five-million-dollar Matisse from the Gleaberg Museum of Art in Nashville."

"Are you sure it was Nick?" she asked, watching as Ryerson called in the troops and cuffed Mr. Ray-Bans.

"I've just texted you a photo from one of the museum's security cameras."

Kate turned her phone on and clicked on MESSAGES. The photo showed a man in an oversize hoodie holding a painting under his arm. The man's face was partly obscured by the hood, but she could see enough to recognize Nick.

"I've never seen Nick in a hoodie before," Kate said.

"I'm not interested in his fashion choices," Jessup said.

"You don't understand, sir," Kate said. "Nick shops on Savile Row, not at the outlet mall. He wouldn't wear a hoodie from Old Navy."

"He was trying to blend in with the local yokels."

"How did he steal the painting?"

"He walked into the museum in broad daylight and took it off the wall."

"Where's the fun in that?"

"He got away with it, didn't he?"

"Yes, but that's not why he steals or swindles. It's all about the challenge of the crime or the person he's targeting. What's the point of just lifting a painting? Anybody could do that."

"Maybe he lacks impulse control," Jessup said. "The reason doesn't matter. What matters is that he did it. He broke our deal."

"It doesn't add up. If he wanted to break the deal, he'd pull off something really big, an ambitious hustle with a payoff in the hundreds of millions of dollars. This is small-time."

"Five million dollars isn't small-time to me," Jessup said. "We've kept him too busy to pull off anything more elaborate. So he grabbed the low-hanging fruit."

Kate thought about it as she looked through the bank's double glass doors. The strike team agents, guns drawn and wearing Kevlar vests, were converging on a BMW and pulling a man out of the driver's seat. Five million dollars would probably be a dream score for the three guys they were arresting today, but not to a master criminal like Nick Fox. He'd had the chance to run off with a half billion dollars during their first assignment together, and he'd resisted the temptation. This felt wrong. Not to mention he'd just called, and she assumed that this theft was the thing he hadn't done.

"Nick is smart and discreet," she said. "Why would he let himself be caught on camera?"

"To give us the finger. The Gleaberg is only a block from the Davidson County Sheriff's Office. He's really rubbing our nose in it."

This was the first aspect of the crime that felt to Kate like a Nick Fox caper. It took chutzpah to take a painting from a museum so close to hundreds of cops. Even so, she wasn't sold.

"I want you to get on a plane to Nashville and take him down fast," Jessup said, ending the call.

Kate blew out a sigh, hung up the desk phone, and stuffed her iPhone into her pocket. She looked down at Slick, who was still on his back, bleeding from his nose. His eyes were open but unfocused.

"Hey," she said to him. "Are you okay?"

"I don't know. How do I look?"

"Like a train wreck." She stuck his gun under her waistband and yanked him to his feet. "Let's go."

Kate turned Slick over to the strike team and joined Ryerson.

"So what's the big crisis?" Ryerson asked.

She pulled her phone out and showed Ryerson the photo. "Fox has come out into the open again."

"Lucky you."

Kate walked to her car, a white Crown Vic police interceptor she'd bought at an LAPD auction. Like many FBI agents, she kept a go bag, a packed duffel bag of clothes and toiletries, in the trunk. The duffel bag had been in there for three months and her clothes probably smelled like her spare tire, but she could head straight to LAX and catch the next flight to Nashville. Before that happened, she needed to talk to Nick.

He answered on the second ring. "Remington Steele, at your service."

"Remington Steele? You've got to be kidding."

"Is it too on the nose?"

"I thought you were James Bond today."

"I'm trying to keep things interesting."

"My fear is that you're trying to keep things *too* interesting."

"Everything I've done lately I've done with you," Nick said.

"Not everything."

"Not for lack of trying. But a man has his needs."

There was a time not so long ago when Fox's sexual banter annoyed Kate. Now she was annoyed to find that she was enjoying it.

"Where are you?" she asked him.

"On my yacht."

"You have a yacht?"

"I do this week," he said.

"I suppose you're somewhere with clear blue skies and no extradition treaty."

"Marina del Rey."

"Really?"

"Come see for yourself," he said, and gave her the slip number.

2

The gleaming Italian-made yacht at the end of the dock was eighty feet long with sweeping, forward-striving curves that expressed wealth and an urgent desire to keep moving. Nick was standing on the flybridge, sipping a glass of champagne, watching Kate march down the deck. There was an easygoing, natural elegance about him, accented by his aviator shades, white linen shirt, salt-washed chinos, and the sea breeze ruffling his brown hair. He didn't look like a man expecting to be hauled back to prison.

Kate reached the yacht and looked up at him. "Where did you get this?"

"It belongs to a playboy sheik whose hobby is spending his family's oil money making movies. This is where he stays when he comes to L.A. to play producer. I'm yacht-sitting for him."

"Does he know that?"

"No, but I'm sure it would give him enormous peace of mind knowing someone was taking good care of his boat."

She came on board and met him on the flybridge, which was outfitted with a wet bar, a grill, and a U-shaped lounge that wrapped around a teak table on which a platter of shrimp was set.

"What's your connection to the sheik?" she asked, accepting a glass of champagne.

"He invested in one of my movies."

"You don't make movies."

"That was the fun of getting him to invest." He gestured to her outfit with his glass. "You look like a banker who is very proud of her assets."

"I was undercover," Kate said.

"No doubt springing a trap for the Businessman Bandits. Did you get them?"

"Yep." She took a shrimp from the platter on the teak table and dabbed it in some cocktail sauce. "How did you know that's who I was after?"

"I like to keep current."

He stole a glance at her cleavage just as she accidentally dropped a shrimp tail into it.

"Nice catch," Nick said, grinning.

Kate looked down at herself, retrieved the shrimp tail, and tossed it into the water. "I knew these breasts would come in handy someday. I assume you know about the theft of a Matisse in Nashville yesterday?"

"It's what I didn't do. The theft was a crime of opportunity. High-end shoplifting."

Kate showed him the cellphone with his picture on it. "That's you in the picture."

"That's someone *disguised* as me, ruining my reputation."

"And framing you for a crime."

He waved that off. "I'm already a wanted man. What bothers me is that this heist makes me seem desperate and sloppy. This is obviously a ploy to send the FBI in the wrong direction while the thief makes a clean getaway. But it shouldn't be too hard for us to catch him."

"There is no 'us' on this." She put the phone back in her pocket. "I'll handle it."

"It's my good name that he smeared."

"You don't have a good name, and the last place you should be right now is in Nashville, where everyone with a badge is looking for you."

She understood, though, why he was willing to take the risk. He was thinking like a con man and thief, not someone who was secretly working for the FBI. In Nick's profession, his status within the underworld came from his crimes and the word of mouth they generated among his peers and, to a greater degree, those less skilled than he. His status was important because it determined the quality of crew he could recruit and the buyers he could line up on those rare occasions when he wanted to sell what he stole.

"You need my help to catch him," Nick said.

"No, I don't. Catching bad guys is what I do," she said. "I caught you, remember?"

"You just love reminding me of that."

"I certainly do," she said, helping herself to another shrimp.

Kate called Jessup on the way to LAX and told him she believed Nick was being set up. The fact that Nick wasn't on the run, and that she'd found him in L.A. on a big-bucks yacht belonging to a former mark, made it much easier for her to convince her boss that she was right.

"I'm relieved to hear Nick didn't do it," Jessup said. "We've had a lot of success with your covert operation. I'd hate to shut it down now. I want you to find the joker who did this, and do it fast. The Nashville field office is expecting you and will give you all the resources you need."

Kate caught a nonstop flight to Nashville at 2:30 P.M. and spent the four-hour flight thinking about the stolen Matisse.

In her experience, there were two motives for stealing a masterpiece. Money and ownership.

Sometimes the thief stole the painting because it was worth a fortune. This kind of criminal frequently acted on impulse and had no clue how to sell the stolen art. Guys like this usually got caught very quickly. If they didn't get caught, they'd end up stashing the painting in their garage, tossing it in a dumpster, or anonymously returning it. Someone like that wouldn't go to the trouble to masquerade as Nick Fox.

Other times the thief stole the painting intending to immediately ransom it back to the owners or the insurance company. This was perhaps the most common approach, and it often succeeded for the thief. Collectors were often more desperate for the paintings than they were for justice. Once the owners had been contacted, they would make the payoff and keep the FBI in the dark until they got their painting back.

Art was also stolen for collateral. Kate knew that cash-strapped crooks stole enormously valuable paintings to use as collateral in drug and weapons deals. An unframed canvas was like a truck full of gold bars, only much lighter to carry and easier to move across borders. Paintings used like this could bounce around the black market for years without ever ending up on anyone's wall. When they did turn up, it was as an unexpected find during police raids on gangs, terrorists, or drug and arms dealers.

And there were the made-to-order heists. Some outrageously wealthy and powerful people had shopping lists of famous works of art they wanted for their personal, very private, collections. Once they got their hands on a masterpiece, it would never be seen again. Kate and Nick had recently brought down someone like that in an elaborate sting.

The second motive, and one that was rarely encountered, was ownership. The thief stole the painting for his own collection. Nick was sometimes that kind of thief.

And now that she thought about it, she realized Nick was a unique thief with a third motive. Nick stole because it was fun and exciting, and because he was good at it.

So what was the motive for this heist? The thief had stolen the painting like an amateur acting out of greed, taking something valuable because it was within easy reach. But masquerading as Nick Fox showed a high level of sophistication, and a knowledge of the players in the big leagues of crime. That didn't fit the greed scenario.

If the painting was stolen for ransom, then the museum had already heard from the thieves, or they would soon. She'd have to keep the key administrators under watch for any suspicious activity.

Someone taking the painting for collateral wouldn't waste time on creative flourishes like setting up Nick. They cared only about the painting and what it could bring them in a trade. Super-rich people with shopping lists of masterpieces wanted discretion from their thieves and wouldn't appreciate the glance at the camera, even if it was intended as misdirection. So she ruled out theft-to-order.

If she took money off the table for now, then the only motive left was ownership, which meant the thief was a world-class criminal in the same rarified league as Nick. And that made her wonder if Nick knew more about the crime than he was telling.

"It's hard for me to feel much sympathy for Big Mike," FBI Special Agent Maxine Cutler said.

Cutler was driving Kate to the FBI's Nashville field office, located two miles north of the airport. Cutler had been waiting at the gate when the plane arrived at 8:45 P.M. She was a big-boned woman in her thirties who looked like she could toss a manhole cover as easily as a Frisbee.

"Who's Big Mike?" Kate asked.

"Michael Gleaberg," Cutler said. "It's his museum that got hit. Serves him right. He discovered and managed some of the biggest country music stars of the seventies and eighties and got stinking rich off them. He looked for kids with lots of talent and no education so they'd foolishly sign contracts that gave him everything but their souls. Big Mike made them famous by bribing DJs to play their songs. He was at the center of a huge payola scandal in the late nineties, but the Bureau couldn't make any charges stick to him."

They crossed under the I-40 into a neighborhood of warehouses, office buildings, and airport hotels.

"He never greased any palms himself," Cutler said. "He always had his flunkies do it. So his flunkies got jail time, and his company was fined millions and barred from the record business, but he didn't care. His clients were already stars, so he was happy to just sit back and rake in his lion's share of their earnings."

"Which he spent on art," Kate said.

"For a reason." Cutler pulled into the parking lot of a two-story office building. The only things indicating it was a government office were the American and Tennessee flags outside the front door. "The big players on the coasts treated him like a dumb hillbilly. He figured they'd respect a man who had Picassos, Rembrandts, and Matisses hanging in his house."

"Did it work?"

"Nobody came to see them," Cutler said. "So he built the museum, put his best stuff in it, and called it the Gleaberg, mimicking the Getty and the Guggenheim."

"Subtle," Kate said.

"There isn't anything subtle about Big Mike. He wears the biggest Stetson they make and a silver belt buckle the size of a turkey platter." Cutler took the key out of the ignition and handed it to Kate. "This is your vehicle while you're in town. You're staying at the Marriott across the street. If you want a bite and a beer before bed, there's Darfons nearby or fast food down the street. I'll get you checked in with security and give you a quick tour."

The tour ended at a small conference room that had been set aside for Kate and her team. On the table were several thin files, a laptop computer, a USB flash drive, and some yellow legal pads.

"This is all we've got," Cutler said. "The surveillance footage from the museum cameras is on that thumb drive, and those files contain witness statements, though you won't find much there. It happened so fast that nobody paid any attention. No two descriptions of the thief are alike."

Kate sat down, plugged the thumb drive into the laptop, and watched the footage, which was broken up into eight mini-screens representing the feeds from eight cameras. The entrance hall of the museum was bright, modern, and airy, with large windows overlooking the Cumberland River. There wasn't much of a crowd, and spotting the man in the hoodie was easy. He entered the museum with intent, a man who knew where he wanted to go and exactly how he wanted to get there, moving at a precise trajectory that kept his face completely hidden from the cameras at all times.

She followed his path across the screens to the gallery with the Matisse. He went directly to the painting, lifted it carefully off the wall with leather-gloved hands, and walked out with it the way he came. People saw him, but no one seemed to react, perhaps assuming he was an employee of the museum. Who else would dare take a painting off the wall?

As he turned to go, he briefly showed his partially obscured face to the camera. It was meant to come across as a mistake, but Kate knew better. The face was definitely Nick's and the thief had wanted the FBI to see it.

On the screen, she watched the thief hurry outside, where a gray late-model Ford F-150 pickup was waiting on the street. He laid the painting in the truck bed, threw a tarp over it, and drove off. Neither the driver's face, nor the license plate of the truck, were visible from the camera's angle.

She watched the footage several more times over the next hour, studying the man and trying to get a sense of his age, mannerisms, and build. The hoodie was oversize and the jeans were baggy, making it impossible to get a sense of his physique.

He didn't walk like Nick, who seemed relaxed even when he was in a hurry. The man in the hoodie moved quickly, but also with a lightness and grace. Nothing else popped out at her. Either there was nothing there or she was too tired to see it.

Kate turned to Cutler. "How many agents have I got working for me?"

"Five, counting me," Cutler said.

"I want someone on Gleaberg, and whoever runs his museum."

"Alton Pruitt manages the museum. Do you think one of them was in on it?"

"I wouldn't rule it out, but that's not why I want them watched. If there's a ransom demand, either Gleaberg or Pruitt is going to get it and will start acting weird and agitated."

"Gotcha," Cutler said.

"Let's send this video to Quantico for analysis to make sure it hasn't been digitally altered in any way. Next, let's get a run-down on all the Ford F-150 trucks that have been stolen, rented, or sold in the state in the last forty-eight hours."

"Anything else?"

"That'll do it for now."

Kate gathered up the files. She would read the witness statements in her hotel room over a Big Mac Extra Value Meal, but she didn't expect to find anything useful.

3

The Gleaberg Museum of Art looked like a flying saucer that had crashed into a circus tent on the shore of the Cumberland River. The building had been designed by an eccentric Swedish architect who liked bold architectural flourishes that didn't serve any structural purpose. The circular main hall of the Gleaberg was cantilevered over the river and covered under a high-tech white canvas strapped down with massive cables.

Kate met Alton Pruitt, the Gleaberg's curator, in the center of the main hall. He was a lanky man in his forties with his black hair slicked back.

"No offense, Mr. Pruitt," Kate said. "But you don't look like any museum administrator I've ever met."

"I hear that a lot. I'm a frustrated country music singer. I was one of Big Mike's only clients he couldn't make into a star.

So I got a master's degree in art history instead, and here I am. I perform on weekends in a Johnny Cash tribute band at weddings and such."

Kate smiled at that. If she ever got married, she was going to hire this guy to get her down the aisle.

"I've read through the initial police reports," Kate said. "And at the risk of sounding judgmental, it would appear that your security is lacking. The Matisse wasn't attached to an alarm, and you don't have any armed guards."

"If there are armed guards, then there could be a shootout. And what would the result of that be? Bullet holes in people and paintings. We have an alarm system that we set at night. It never occurred to anyone that a painting would walk out of here during the day. We'll fix that by putting guards at all exits."

Kate went back to the FBI field office and spent hours sorting through all the Ford F-150 sales, rentals, and thefts. By nightfall, Kate and her crew had a list of more than a hundred trucks to look for and had located thirteen of them. None of the ones they found had any connection to the theft. She left the office around 8 P.M. and returned to her hotel room.

There was a small television bolted to the dresser but no visible remote. She was going through drawers, looking for the remote, when there was a knock at her door. She gave up on her search, squinted through the peephole, and was shocked to see Carl Jessup standing in the hall.

Her first thought was that he was there to fire her. She could think of no other reason for him to be making a personal appearance. Great. She'd been pretty much kicked out of the Navy, and now she was going to be booted out of the FBI. Okay, fine, but she was keeping the windbreaker.

She pulled herself up tall and opened the door. "It's not often that I see you in the field," Kate said with forced good cheer.

She took a closer look. It wasn't Jessup. It was someone wearing a Jessup mask. Damn! Kate pulled the fake Jessup into her room with one hand, kicked his legs out from under him, and body slammed him to the floor.

"That hurt," the fake Jessup said. "I didn't see that coming. You really have to work on your hostess skills."

Kate looked down at him. "Nick?"

He took the mask off. "I thought I'd surprise you."

She closed and locked the door. "Are you out of your mind? The FBI field office is right across the street."

"Would you prefer I'd visited you there?"

"I would have preferred you didn't visit me at all."

"I find that hard to believe. I'm charming. And I have a show-and-tell for you."

"Don't even think about it."

"Not that kind of show-and-tell," Nick said. "That show-and-tell comes later. I brought you a mask."

"Of course," Kate said. "I knew that."

"It's made from a thin layer of hard resin. A computer does a detailed facial reconstruction from just a couple pictures and then sculpts the mask in a 3-D printer. It's ridiculously easy to get a mask like this. You can order one online for three hundred dollars and have it delivered to your door in forty-eight hours. Of course, I can get it done faster."

"You could have told me this on the phone. You didn't have to come here."

"True, but I miss you when you're gone."

Kate's heart skipped a beat. He missed her! Oh good grief, she thought. Get a grip. He's a con man!

Nick looked around the room. "I'm starved. Where's the minibar?"

"This room doesn't have a minibar."

Nick kicked his shoes off and stretched out on the bed, hands behind his head. "We need to change hotels. I have standards."

"*You* need to change hotels. I'm fine. I have no standards."

Nick grinned and crooked his finger at her. "Come here. I like a woman with no standards."

Kate squinched her eyes closed and grunted. "Unh!" She opened one eye and studied him. "What do you know about the Gleaberg robbery that you aren't telling me?"

"Nothing," he said. "But I've done some business with Big Mike. A few years ago, right after his payola scandal, I got him to invest in a phony satellite radio network on the promise that his artists would get airplay."

"He went for that?"

"It appealed to his greed and his desire to win. He was still angry about being locked out of the terrestrial radio business, but there was nothing in the court's ruling that kept him from satellite radio. The deal I offered made him feel like he was getting back at the bastards who took him down. He was the perfect mark. Rich, dishonest, and greedy."

"How much did you and your crew take him for?"

"Fifteen million dollars," Nick said.

"He never reported it to the police or FBI."

"Of course not," Nick said. "It was humiliating. The wealthier the mark, the less likely he is to go to the police and admit he was played for a fool."

They went silent when someone knocked on the door.

"Room service?" Nick asked in a whisper.

Kate shook her head no.

There was another knock. "Agent O'Hare? It's Maxine Cutler."

Nick grabbed his shoes and the Jessup mask, moved into the closet, and closed the door.

Kate unlatched the security lock and peeked out at Cutler.

"Can I come in?" Cutler asked. "It's important."

"Sure," Kate said, stepping aside.

"We got a bulletin from Interpol," Cutler said. "Nick Fox has struck again. He stole an ancient goblet covered with jewels from the Aykut Demirkan Museum in Istanbul last night."

"How do they know it was Fox?"

"They lifted his prints from a display case." Cutler handed Kate an envelope. "Your boss works fast. He has you on an early morning flight to Istanbul. The Bureau's legal attaché for Asia has already approved your travel with Turkish authorities. Your itinerary and boarding passes are in the envelope."

Kate did a fast check of the boarding passes and inwardly groaned. Sixteen hours with two plane changes. Coach.

"I'll drop off the car and my weapon with the field office at five A.M.," she said to Cutler. "If you could have someone take me to the airport, I'd appreciate it."

Cutler left, and Nick reappeared from out of the closet.

"About the fingerprints," she said.

Kate knew that making fake fingerprints was easy. Kits could be bought online from China for as little as six dollars. The trick was getting Nick's prints in the first place. A law enforcement officer could access the FBI's Integrated Automated Fingerprint Identification System to see the prints taken from Nick when he was arrested. But unless the IAFIS had been hacked, which nobody had succeeded in doing yet, there would be a log of anyone accessing Nick's prints. She'd check that out, but she doubted she'd find any record of access besides the one initiated by Turkish law enforcement to match the print found at the Aykut Demirkan Museum. So that left only one possibility.

"Whoever is doing this got close enough to you at some point to get your fingerprints from you or from something you touched," Kate said.

Nick flopped back onto the bed. "That narrows it down to every bartender, waitress, and hotel housekeeper I've ever encountered."

"Why the goblet?" Kate asked. "What does the goblet have in common with the Gleaberg painting?"

"Nothing, other than me."

"Do not leave the United States until this is over," Kate told him. "Go into hiding. Act as if you're a fugitive on the FBI's Ten Most Wanted list. That shouldn't be too hard for you . . . *since you are number seven.*"

4

Kate awoke just as the Turkish Airlines plane began its early morning descent to Atatürk Airport. Far below her the Bosphorus Strait divided the historic city of Istanbul. Europe was to the west and Asia to the east.

She was traveling light with just her duffel bag, so she deplaned and went straight to Customs. She showed the officer her brown FBI passport, which notified authorities that she was on official business. The agent eyed her suspiciously for a few long seconds, stamped her documents, and motioned her through.

Kate had been told that someone would meet her just past Customs. She expected it would be a driver from the Turkish police or the U.S. Consulate. The man holding the iPad with her name on it was neither of those. He wore a black fez, dark sunglasses, a white turtleneck shirt, and a black Nehru jacket with a flowered emblem on the breast pocket. The emblem was a tulip with a curved dagger for a stem.

With the exception of the iPad, Kate thought he could have passed for a Turkish assassin in a cheesy 1960s spy movie. In which case there would be another assassin in a fez hiding behind a pillar, waiting to kill her with a blow dart if the turtleneck killer failed. And then a handsome man would pop up to save her. Indiana Jones.

The turtleneck killer approached her. "Welcome to Istanbul, Bayan O'Hare." He tucked the iPad under one arm and reached for her duffel bag with the other. "I am Erdin. I will take you to the Aykut Demirkan Museum."

"I was expecting someone from the Turkish police or the U.S. Consulate to meet me."

"I work for the Demirkan Foundation. Chief Investigator Semir Atalay of the Emniyet Genel Müdürlüğü, our police department, and Bayan Ceren Demirkan, the director of the Foundation, are awaiting you at the museum. They are most eager to see you. Please come along."

Kate followed him out of the building and onto the tarmac, where a black helicopter was waiting. The tulip and dagger emblem was splashed across its side, and a red carpet led to the steps. They boarded without ceremony, and the helicopter lifted up and headed out over the Bosphorus.

Erdin pointed out the Blue Mosque, the Hagia Sophia, and Topkapi Palace. "These are our national treasures," he said, his voice coming through Kate's headset. "They were long ago constructed as symbols of faith, wealth, and power. They are now open to the public."

"I know all about them," Kate said. "I saw a special on the Travel Channel, but they're even more amazing in person, with the morning sun shining on them."

The chopper followed the Bosphorus Strait toward a huge suspension bridge. Just before they reached the bridge, the helicopter veered sharply to the west, and flew over a large waterfront villa.

"This is the Aykut Demirkan Museum," Erdin told Kate. "It's in a *yali,* a summer house that has belonged to the Demirkans for many generations."

Kate had grown up on a bunch of army bases, and her summer house experience was a tent in the woods. The Demirkan summer house was huge. Four stories, with ornate marble and gold trimmings.

The helicopter fluttered down onto the lawn, not far from a tall woman wearing a white dress and a short man in an ill-fitting gray suit. The welcoming committee, Kate thought, waiting for the helicopter to wind down before she disembarked and walked to the man and woman.

"I'm Special Agent Kate O'Hare," she said, offering her hand to the man, who had a high, shiny brow and a wispy gray-flecked goatee.

"Chief Inspector Atalay," he said. "I look forward to working with you." He turned toward the woman beside him. "This is

Ceren Demirkan. She runs her family's foundation, which owns this museum and the collection it contains."

Ceren offered her hand. She had long, delicate fingers, and pale, glowing skin that gave the middle-aged woman an almost ethereal quality.

"I'm so glad you're here," Ceren said. "I understand you're *the* expert on Nicolas Fox."

"I've spent a lot of years chasing him," Kate said.

"You are also the only one who has ever captured him. And if you did it once, you can do it again."

Kate was beginning to see the dynamic at work here, and why the Bureau's legal attaché had been able to clear her travel so quickly. Ceren thought Kate was the one and only magician who could snag Fox and reclaim the lost goblet. Chief Inspector Atalay didn't look as convinced.

Ceren led Kate and Atalay to the museum.

"I'm sure you've noticed the family crest displayed everywhere," Ceren said. "The tulip symbolizes the flowering of culture, art, and architecture in the Ottoman Empire during the fifteenth and sixteenth centuries, the period represented by the majority of the pieces in our collection. Our ancient ancestor Aykut Demirkan was a *sipahi,* what you'd consider a medieval knight. It is by virtue of his fortitude, bravery, and business acumen that our family grew and spread across Europe, much like the tulip. The *kilij,* or saber, represents our family's, and our foundation's, enduring patriotism, strength, and determination."

Ceren walked past the main entrance and took them to the side of the building where police tape cordoned off an area around a fire exit. The steel double doors appeared to have been forced open. An armed uniformed police officer guarded the door.

"This is where Nicolas Fox broke in two nights ago," Chief Inspector Atalay said. "He forced open the door with a crowbar."

The nature of the crime matched the simplistic approach of the Gleaberg job, Kate thought. It bore no resemblance to the audacious, precisely planned heists that were the trademark of Nick Fox.

"Where were the guards and patrols?" Kate asked.

"There weren't any," Ceren replied. "Naturally, we have guards during the day when people are going through the museum and could steal or vandalize items in the collection. But at night, we rely upon state-of-the-art alarm systems that include motion detectors, heat sensors, infrared beams, and complete video surveillance of the interior and exterior of the building. All the alarms worked perfectly and the police were here within five minutes, but by then it was already over."

"Have you looked at the video?"

The line of Ceren's mouth tightened. "There isn't any video. It was disconnected a while back during a service call, and was never put back on line."

"Oops," Kate said.

Atalay nodded. "An unfortunate oversight, but at least we

know the thief arrived and escaped by boat. We would have cut him off on our way here if he was using any other kind of vehicle or if he was on foot. There's only one road leading to this museum."

Atalay opened the door, and the three of them went inside. They climbed a few steps and walked through another door into a gallery with a low ceiling and walls covered with mosaic tiles. The shattered display case was in the center of the gallery, surrounded by jeweled artifacts, including piles of gold coins, housed in other cases around the room. There were ornamental vases on pedestals as well.

"Tell me about the cup that was taken," Kate said to Ceren.

"It was a jewel-encrusted goblet," Ceren said. "It belonged to Sultan Suleiman the Magnificent. He first drank from it to mark the settlement in 1555 of the Ottoman-Safavid war that granted him rule of Baghdad, and the mouths of the Euphrates and Tigris rivers. The goblet has incalculable historical importance."

Kate knew the Demirkan wasn't the first private museum to rely entirely on their alarm systems for after-hours security. The Kunsthal in Rotterdam made the same decision. They had been robbed a couple years before of seven paintings worth more than $130 million in just two minutes. The thieves were caught, but the mother of one of them incinerated several paintings in a tragic effort to get rid of the evidence.

"This isn't Fox's style," Kate said. "Everything I know about him tells me this isn't his work."

"We found Fox's fingerprint on a shard of glass inside the display case," Atalay said.

"That's another reason why I don't think it's him," Kate said. "He's not that sloppy."

"He was in a hurry," Atalay said. "He knew he couldn't beat the security system, so he gave up, and ignored the sensors, setting them off. He knew that would give him only two or three minutes before we descended on the museum in force. People make mistakes under that kind of pressure."

"He wouldn't put himself in that situation," Kate said.

"Unless he was desperate," Atalay said. "And I think it's fair to say that he probably is desperate. He's been on the run for a year since his escape."

She could have told him he was wrong, that Nick's escape was planned by the FBI, and that he was now working for the U.S. government . . . sort of. But she didn't. This was highly classified information.

"If there is anything either of you need to pursue your investigation," Ceren said, "the full resources of the Demirkan Foundation are at your disposal."

Atalay and Ceren exchanged a few words in Turkish, Ceren walked away, and the chief inspector motioned for Kate to come with him.

"Come along," he said. "Let us get some breakfast."

5

Kate and Atalay walked to a little café facing the Bosphorus, got a table by the window, and Atalay ordered in Turkish for both of them. The waiter served them *çay,* a hot tea in tiny glasses, and went off to place their order with the cook.

"The Demirkans are a very rich, very politically connected family in Turkey," Atalay said. "They were informed that the fingerprint on the glass belonged to Nicolas Fox before I was assigned to investigate the case. By the time I was told, they had already learned about you and made sure that Interpol alerted the FBI about Fox. They also pressured the Turkish government to instantly grant the FBI's request to send you here. So, you see, you are in charge, Agent O'Hare. I am here to help you in any way possible."

"It's exactly the opposite," Kate said. "This is your city and your investigation. I'll offer you what I know about Fox, and my opinion if I think it might help, but I won't get in your way. I'm an interested observer."

He smiled, clearly relieved. "My friends call me Semir."

Kate relaxed back in her chair. "And I'm Kate. So, Semir, I know this messes things up for you, but I'll say this again. I'm pretty sure Fox didn't do this. I think this is the work of an imposter."

"It doesn't matter whether it was Nicolas Fox or Michael J. Fox. Whoever did it is long gone."

"You know who Michael J. Fox is?"

"Of course I do. This is Istanbul, not Siberia, though I am sure they've seen *Back to the Future* there, too."

"What makes you so sure the thief isn't in Istanbul any-more?"

Atalay gestured to the Bosphorus. "Look out there, Kate. Tell me what you see."

Kate looked out at the strait. It was bustling with fishing boats, tour boats, ferries, cruise ships, freighters, patrol boats, barges, and just about every other kind of oceangoing vessel that existed, with the possible exceptions of an aircraft carrier and a four-masted Spanish galleon.

"It looks like an L.A. freeway at rush hour," Kate said. "Only with ships."

"For thousands of years, the Bosphorus has been the gateway to the world, which is why Istanbul is here and why it was the capital of three great empires," Atalay said. "Once the thief was out there on the water, he could have met with a ship bound for anywhere. I'm sure that's what he did. It's what I would do."

The waiter came back with a platter of cheeses, bread and olives, a skillet of fried eggs with dried spicy sausage, flat bread rolled and stuffed with meat and cheese, a sweet pastry filled with potato, and a square of clotted cream served with honey on fresh bread.

Kate dug in, and while she ate she thought about the parallels between the Gleaberg and Demirkan thefts, and the heavy-handed way Nick was being set up. It made her wonder how well the thief really knew Nick, and how closely he was following Nick's old MO.

"I imagine you are under a lot of pressure to produce results," Kate said to Atalay as the waiters cleared their plates and brought them tiny cups of Turkish coffee. "What steps are you taking to investigate the crime?"

"We are looking into stolen boats that the thief might have used to reach the Demirkan and make his escape. It's a fruitless exercise, I am sure. We are also talking to the usual suspects— the former thieves, the suspected thieves, the people who sell the things that thieves take—to see what they know. But they will know nothing. We are also seeking people who have the means, and the desire, to own an object like the goblet. It is a very small group, but they will not talk. They have lawyers and functionaries to talk and lie for them. We are also questioning jewelers on the chance the thief might have been greedy and ignorant and stolen the goblet just for the stones. If that is the case, he will have to go to these jewelers to sell the stones he has pried off the piece. That prospect is too frightening to think about."

He was like the Eeyore of cops, seeing only failure and gloom, Kate thought, staring down at her coffee. It was so thick, she wasn't sure whether she was supposed to drink it or eat it like pudding.

"There's a long shot we could try," she said. "I'd like you to get the guest lists from all of the four- and five-star hotels in the city and the passenger lists of all the flights, trains, buses, and boats arriving and departing from Istanbul over the last four days, and then send them to my colleagues at the FBI."

"What can they do with the information that we can't?"

"Fox likes to use the names of TV characters as aliases. I have a contact who will compare your lists with names in *The Complete Directory of Episodic Television Shows.*"

"Those names would be meaningless to most people here, so I can see why he'd choose one," Atalay said. "But wouldn't it be wiser for him to choose places to stay that are less conspicuous than five-star hotels?"

"Fox likes the finer things in life."

"Who doesn't? Getting the airline, train, bus, and boat passenger lists will take a day at least, maybe two. I can get the hotel guest lists today, but it will take a few hours. This is a big city with many fine hotels." He glanced at his watch and did a quick mental calculation. "If we get the guest lists by midafternoon, that means it will be ready first thing in the morning for your colleagues in the U.S."

"That would be terrific."

Atalay and Kate finished their coffees and walked back to the museum, where a uniformed police officer was waiting to drive Kate to her hotel.

"I would go to the station with you to help with the investigation, but I suspect I would only be in the way," Kate said to Atalay.

"This is true. Unless you speak Turkish and have contacts in the Istanbul underworld, there is not much for you to do right now."

Kate checked into her hotel, changed out of her wrinkled suit, and set out to be a tourist. She bypassed Topkapi Palace and the Blue Mosque, choosing instead to walk the congested, winding side streets. She ate food from street vendors, had another coffee, and browsed through the shops and outdoor stalls.

Shortly after five, she returned to her small boutique hotel in the Old City. It was located on a narrow side street that came to a dead end behind a mosque. The *ezan*, the late afternoon call to prayer, was being broadcast from speakers mounted on the mosque's minarets. The melodic chant, which summoned devout Muslims to the mosque six times each day, was so loud that she almost didn't hear her phone ringing. It was Chief Inspector Atalay calling to tell her that he had the list of hotel guests and that he would be right over. Twenty minutes later, Atalay and four of his men pulled up outside the hotel in two unmarked cars. Kate met them on the street and took the list from Atalay.

"I sent the original list in to your colleague Maxine Cutler, as you suggested," Atalay said. "This one I just handed you is the list she sent back after checking in the television book. There are twenty-three names."

The number of hits didn't surprise Kate. Most TV character names aren't as unique as Thomas Magnum, Napoleon Solo, or Horatio Caine. She quickly scanned the list, which included Robert Ewing, Michael Brady, Alex Keaton, Fred Sanford, and Alan Shore. One name jumped out at her. Dale Cooper, the FBI agent Kyle MacLachlan had played on *Twin Peaks*. It was exactly the kind of name that Nick would have chosen back in the days when she was chasing him.

"Dale Cooper could be our man," Kate said. "Which hotel gave you his name?"

"The Four Seasons," Atalay said. "It's right up the street, in the old prison."

"Really? A prison?" She felt a twinge of excitement in her chest. "You must be joking."

"It's true. Sultanahmet Prison was one of the most notorious and feared places in our country. It was where political prisoners, mostly writers and journalists, were sent to rot. Now it's a five-star luxury hotel, where people pay top dollar to stay in former dungeons. Amazing, isn't it?"

The irony would be irresistible to Nick. If he ever came to Istanbul, she knew the Four Seasons Turkish prison was definitely where he'd stay. And if someone was trying to imitate him, they might stay there as well.

"Let's talk to the desk clerk at the Four Seasons," Kate said. "Have your men drive there and park near the front and rear exits. Tell them to stay out of sight. We don't want to spook our suspect on the off chance that he's there. And if he isn't there we might still learn something helpful."

Atalay leaned in the window of the car and gave the driver orders in Turkish. The cars turned around at the end of the street and headed back the way they came. Atalay and Kate began their short walk up the cobblestoned street.

Despite the yellow paint, red-tile roof, ocher-tinted masonry, and white balustrades along the terraces and walls, the hotel's origins as a prison were obvious. The building had high walls with tall guard towers at two corners. The entrance was grand but imposing, with bars on the windows. The three flagpoles along the front wall added a touch of governmental authority to the place.

"There are sixty-five suites," Atalay said as they neared the front entrance. "The guard towers are occupied by elevators, and the former exercise yard is now a garden with a fancy restaurant. But the fact that it was once a prison works to our benefit if we get lucky and Fox or his imposter is still here. There aren't a lot of exits. It will be easy for us to lock down."

"Don't get your hopes up," Kate said, more to caution herself than Atalay. She was on the hunt and she felt a small drip, drip, drip of adrenaline flow into her system. There was a chance that the thief was still in Istanbul. And if he wasn't still here, the desk clerk might remember him. Plus there were security cameras everywhere. Surely Dale Cooper didn't always wear his Nick Fox mask.

They stepped into a marble foyer and walked down a long corridor of high arches. The registration desk was at the end of the passageway. Across from the registration desk was a wall lined with small windows that looked out onto the former prison yard and the opposite wing of the hotel.

The desk clerk was a young man with posture so rigid and straight he made the marble pillars around him appear crooked. He greeted them in Turkish. Atalay flashed his identification, introduced himself, and then spoke in English for Kate's sake.

"We're looking for a man named Dale Cooper," Atalay said. "We believe he was registered here."

The desk clerk went to his computer. "Dale Cooper reserved a suite yesterday, but checked in just a couple hours ago."

That didn't make sense to Kate. The break-in at the museum was committed two nights ago. Why would the thief check in to the hotel today?

And then, with an overwhelming sense of dread, the answer hit her at precisely the same moment that Atalay pulled a photo of Nick from his shirt pocket and showed it to the clerk.

"Is this him?" Atalay asked.

The clerk gave the picture a quick glance and nodded. "Yes, that's Mr. Cooper."

Of course it was, Kate thought. Because the real Nick Fox had come to Istanbul despite her warnings and got a room exactly where she thought he would. She knew Nick all too well. And now she'd led the Turkish police right to the man she was supposed to protect.

Atalay took out his cellphone, dialed a number, gave some quick commands in Turkish, and turned to Kate. "I've told my men to secure the exits and to call for backup, all in plainclothes. If Fox is in this hotel, he's not getting out."

But if Nick wasn't in the hotel, Atalay had made a grave mistake. Nick had a sixth sense about law enforcement. He'd easily spot the detectives on the street no matter how they were dressed, and he'd go back the way he came. She hoped that's what would happen. The alternative was that he was still in the hotel, already a prisoner without knowing it.

"What room is Cooper in?" Atalay asked the clerk.

"Room 302, a deluxe suite."

The clerk took out a sheet of paper printed with the floor plan of the hotel and circled the room. It was two doors down from the stairs and had windows that looked out over the courtyard and restaurant.

Atalay and Kate went to the lobby's courtyard windows and looked up at the third-floor room. The sheers were drawn, but the lights were on.

The chief inspector stepped back behind the wall for cover and told Kate his plan. Once his men arrived, he'd position detectives at the stairs and elevators on every floor. He and a team of men would go up to the third floor and flank the door to room 302. At that point, Atalay would send a text to his man in the lobby instructing him to have the desk clerk make a courtesy call to Nick's room.

"The clerk will say he's calling Fox to see if there's anything else the Four Seasons can do to make his stay more enjoyable," Atalay said. "Not that it matters what he says. I will be close enough to the door to hear the phone ring. The second Fox picks up, we'll burst in and take him. And if he's not in the room, then all of us will pull back out of sight and wait for him to show up."

"It's a good plan," Kate said. In fact, it was probably what she'd do herself in the same situation. The problem was that it could succeed.

"You need to stay out of sight," Atalay said to Kate. "If he sees you, we're finished. You will have to wait here."

The translation was that Atalay didn't want a woman he barely knew along on a mission that might include a firefight, Kate thought. This was fine by her since her primary goal now was to warn Nick, and she needed a private moment to do it.

Almost immediately, a dozen other plainclothes detectives arrived. Atalay assigned them to areas around the hotel, stationed one at the front desk, and then took the three remaining men with him up to the third floor.

That left Kate alone in the lobby with two desk clerks and the detective, a man named Giray. He had his phone out and ready, waiting for instructions from Atalay.

Kate stepped behind a pillar, took out her phone, and sent a one-word text to Nick. *RUN.*

Giray's phone dinged with the arrival of Atalay's text and he gave the go-ahead nod to the clerk, who picked up the phone and made the call to Nick's room.

"Here we go," Giray said to Kate with a heavy Turkish accent.

They walked into the courtyard and looked up at Nick's third-floor room. The window opened, and Nick Fox casually climbed out. Giray cursed and called Atalay.

Kate was trying to stay calm, but her heart was pounding in her chest. Nick was on a narrow ledge, and he was reaching for a drainpipe. It was an arm's length away, and it didn't look all that sturdy. Kate closed her eyes and wished she was Catholic so she could ask God for a favor. She opened her eyes and saw that Nick had made it onto the drainpipe and was shimmying up to the roof.

Atalay's head popped out of Nick's open window. He leaned forward and aimed his gun at Nick. "Halt," Atalay said.

Nick looked down at Atalay. "Give me a good reason."

"I'll shoot you if you don't."

"If you shoot me, and I fall to my death, you'll never find the goblet."

Atalay said something in Turkish, and Kate looked to Giray for a translation.

"Very bad word," Giray said. "A lady would not like it."

Atalay climbed halfway out the window and stopped. He looked at the drainpipe and then at the street. It was a long drop down if he didn't connect with the pipe. He ducked back into the room, and Kate heard him shout instructions to his men.

She tipped her head back and watched Nick do a slow run across the rooftop toward the terrace that ran the length of the next wing. It was easy to underestimate him, she thought. He had a hidden athleticism. His body was perfectly hinged together, and he had the muscle tone and coordination of a cat. How he stayed so toned was a mystery since she never saw him work out. She told herself it was wrong, wrong, wrong to look that hot while breaking the law, but that didn't alter the fact that he *was* breaking the law, and he *was* damn sexy up there on the roof, backlit by the twilight sky.

He slid down the slanted end of the roof, dropped onto a third-floor terrace, and disappeared inside the building. Kate dashed back to the lobby and joined a half dozen Turkish cops who were running toward the main entrance. Everyone burst out of the hotel onto the street and gave a collective gasp. Fox was standing on the second floor balustrade. He jumped onto one of the three flagpoles in front of the hotel and, without missing a beat, he flung himself onto the roof of a passing minibus. The minibus sped down the hill into the warren of narrow streets that led to the waterfront.

Kate thought of the old adage that sometimes it was better to be lucky than to be good. In Nick Fox's case, he was both.

Some of the cops scrambled for their cars while others gave chase on foot. Kate was part of the foot chase, sprinting down the narrow street and around a corner. She saw Nick crouch on the roof of the minibus and jump for a balcony on a crumbling old building. He hoisted himself over the railing and disappeared inside.

The police ran into the building through a shoe store, but Kate remained outside and waited. She heard dogs barking, people yelling, and things crashing. A moment later, Nick appeared on a neighboring rooftop. He was wearing a long coat and a Fedora that he'd pilfered somewhere along the way. He looked like some kind of superhero, his long coat fluttering like a cape. Nick blew Kate a kiss and dashed away again along the rooftops and into the creeping darkness.

Atalay ran up beside her just as Nick disappeared. "How did he know that we were coming?"

Kate stared resolutely at the rooftop where Nick had stood. "There were a lot of cops outside the Four Seasons. Someone may have come to meet with Fox, got spooked by what he saw, and warned him. It doesn't matter *how* it happened, only that it *did*. He's very clever."

6

The manhunt in the Old City continued fruitlessly until Atalay finally called it off at midnight.

Kate trudged back to her hotel and up to her third-floor room, which was barely large enough to hold the four-poster bed. The pillows on the bed were flat, and there was only a single rough top sheet. As an ex–Navy commando, she'd slept on much worse. She wasn't sleeping on rocks, and as far as she knew she wasn't sleeping with scorpions, so it was all good. She was asleep ten seconds after her head hit the pillow.

She was awakened at 3:30 in the morning by the call to prayer from the mosque, and it took her another hour to fall asleep again, only to be awakened a little over two hours later by the dawn call to prayer.

She lay in bed for another forty-five minutes, mulling over

what investigative steps she could take next to flush out the fake Nick without nailing the real one. No brilliant ideas occurred to her, so she showered, got dressed in jeans and a long-sleeved white T-shirt, and went to the rooftop terrace for the hotel's buffet breakfast.

There were already two dozen hotel guests scattered among the long communal tables inside the dining room and at the small tables on the patio. They were eating breakfast, reviewing guidebooks, and taking lots of selfies standing with their backs against the rooftop railing, the panoramic view of the Sea of Marmara behind them.

Kate took a warm plate from the stack at the end of the bar and browsed the offerings on the buffet. She'd tried most of the dishes the previous morning with Atalay. She loaded up on the fried eggs, sausage, fruit, and cheese, picked up a glass of tea, and carried her breakfast to the far end of the table with the worst view and the fewest guests. The last thing she wanted to do was engage in small talk with chatty tourists.

She was working her way through her eggs when a bearded man in a flannel shirt and faded jeans slid onto the bench across from her. His plate was piled so high with food that an avalanche of olives, cubes of cheese, and a portion of bread pudding toppled onto the table when he sat down.

"If there's one thing I love," he said, "it's free grub."

He spoke with an indecipherable American southern accent, a little bit of the Carolinas mixed with backwater Louisiana. He wore a sweat-stained American flag bandana around his head.

His bushy mustache and beard were so thick and mangy, it was like he had a wild animal sitting on his face. The only things she could see clearly behind all of that hair were the tip of his nose and his compelling brown eyes.

"Aren't you afraid someone will recognize your nose?" Kate asked him.

"I'm a risk taker," he said. "What gave me away? Was it the nose?"

"It was the desire to punch you in the face." Kate forked in more eggs and a chunk of sausage. "You lied to me, Nick. You said there wasn't any connection between the heist at the Gleaberg and the one at the Demirkan."

"There isn't."

"But here you are."

"Whither thou goest . . ." he said.

"That's touching, but I suspect there's more."

And actually it *was* touching, Kate thought. Like it or not, even though she wanted to punch him in the face, it was nice to have him across from her at the breakfast table. It was sort of . . . connubial.

"There's curiosity," Nick said.

"So besides me, it's curiosity that got you on a plane?"

"As far as I can see, the only thing the Gleaberg job has in common with the Demirkan is me. And the thief might have my fingerprints, but he isn't thinking like me. I wouldn't come all the way to Istanbul to smash a display case and take a goblet. I'd steal the Topkapi Dagger."

"You can't steal that."

"That's true," he said. "I'd just be repeating myself."

"You never stole the Topkapi Dagger."

"Yes, I did," he said.

The diamond-encrusted dagger, renowned for the three huge emeralds on the grip, was displayed in the Topkapi Palace treasury, a museum full of the amazing riches the sultans acquired during Turkey's reign as the greatest power on earth. It was commonly believed that stealing anything from the treasury was impossible.

"The dagger is one of the world's most famous and coveted treasures," Kate said. "If it had been stolen, I would have heard about it. *Everybody* would have heard about it."

"If anybody noticed," he said. "I swapped the dagger with a fake. Nobody suspected a thing. The next night, I broke into the house of the director general of the Turkish police, and slipped the dagger into his kitchen silverware drawer. He found it when he went to butter his toast for breakfast. Naturally, the police and the palace officials didn't tell a soul about what happened. It would have been too embarrassing."

"Why would you go to the trouble of committing one of the greatest thefts in criminal history only to give back what you stole?"

"Have you ever seen the 1964 movie *Topkapi*?"

"Nope," she said.

"It's one of the best heist flicks ever made. I saw it on TV when I was a kid, and it made a big impression on me. This master thief and a team of amateurs steal the dagger and replace it with a fake. It's the perfect crime, brilliantly conceived and executed, but they're foiled by a tiny twist of fate. I wanted to see if it was possible, despite all the high-tech security measures available today, to actually pull off the heist. Guess what? It is."

"How did you do it?"

Nick shook his head. "I'll never tell."

"I'm not sure I believe that story. But I *do* believe you pulled off a job here that isn't widely known."

Nick selected a piece of salted fish and ate it with bread. "Thanks for the warning last night. I was able to escape with my passports and the complimentary bottle of L'Occitane body lotion in the bathroom." He took the little bottle of L'Occitane out of his shirt pocket and handed it to Kate. "I thought you might like it."

"Thank you. I do like it."

"So what's our next move?" he asked.

"I don't have a next move. Do you have a next move?"

"I'm going to continue to chase the imposter. If the pattern continues, there should be another theft soon that will be attributed to me. This person is sending a message and eventually we'll figure it out."

Kate met Atalay in the police station lobby. The modern five-story glass-cube building might have been impressive had it not been dwarfed by the skyscrapers of Istanbul's New City. Atalay was pacing when Kate walked in, and it was obvious that he'd spent the night in his office. He was in the same clothes he'd worn the day before, his eyes were bloodshot, and his hair looked like a bird's nest.

"I'm guessing you've had a rough night," Kate said. "Has Ceren Demirkan called you yet?"

"She unleashed her fury on the director general," he said. "He wants to see me in his office in ten minutes. I don't think it's to give me a promotion. Not that it matters, because Fox isn't my problem anymore. He has not only eluded us, he's managed to slip out of Istanbul."

"How do you know that?"

"He broke into a billionaire shipping mogul's tenth-floor pied-à-terre in Cologne, Germany, last night and stole a Vermeer out of the man's bedroom while he was sleeping."

"That's not possible," she said.

"A surveillance camera outside a bank across the street got a picture of him leaving the building with the painting tucked under his arm."

"But he couldn't have been there," she said. "We both know he was right here, in the Old City, at six o'clock last night. We saw him with our own eyes."

"If he slipped into a taxi before we were able to seal off the streets, then he could have made it to the airport in time to take a commercial jet to Düsseldorf," Atalay said. "It's only about a three-hour flight, and from there it's only a forty-minute drive to Cologne. Finding Fox is a matter for the Bundeskriminalamt in Germany and Interpol now."

"This shipping mogul?" Kate said. "Was his name Heiko Balz, by any chance? From Berlin?"

"Yes, how did you know?"

"Four years ago, Fox swindled Balz out of a few million euros by selling him a stolen Vermeer that wasn't actually a stolen Vermeer. Or even a Vermeer. Ever since then, Balz has been waiting for Fox to step into Germany so he can get his hands on him."

"Now Fox has a real Vermeer, taken right from under Balz's nose," Atalay said. "Fox has guts, I'll give him that."

That was true, but she couldn't see the reasoning behind any of it. First the fake Nick committed robberies in Nashville and Istanbul that were far less clever than anything the real Nick would do. Now in Cologne, the imposter had robbed Heiko Balz, getting Nick into even more trouble with the mob-connected billionaire. And all three crimes were done in rapid succession, within only a few days of each other. What was the big hurry? Why these three cities? What was the point?

Kate said goodbye to Atalay and walked down the street to a coffeehouse. I'm missing the obvious, Kate thought. This is a connect-the-dots puzzle. You connect the dots and you get to see the picture. My dilemma is that I don't have enough dots yet to guess at the picture, so I'm always a step behind the thief. Truth is, I shouldn't have tried to keep Nick out of this. We probably would have made better progress working together.

Kate went to the counter, ordered a coffee, and took it outside to a small sidewalk table. She sipped the coffee, took a notepad out of her bag, and listed out the robberies. *Big Mike, jeweled goblet, Vermeer.* Nothing clicked in her brain. No brilliant flash of insight. She ran through her conversation with Nick at breakfast. The only thing the Big Mike con and the goblet smash-and-grab have in common is me, he'd said. The *me* was Nick.

Kate wrote *Nick* a bunch of times. She drew a heart around the *Nick*s she'd written. She looked at the heart and was horrified. She scribbled all over the heart until it was unreadable. She wrote *Nashville, Istanbul, Cologne.* Holy crap. There it was in black and white on the paper. It wasn't connect the dots. It was *Wheel of Fortune.* It was fill in the letters and guess the word. And she was pretty sure the word was going to be *Nick* or maybe *Nicolas.* The next city would begin with a *K* or an *O*.

She called Nick and was told the number was no longer in service. Great. She was on her own, and she didn't have much time to make the right educated guess. She searched her memory bank and came up with just one city that fulfilled all the requirements. The French city of Orléans.

Six months before, an alarm sensor system had gone bad on a ground-floor window on the east-facing Rue Fernand Rabier side of the Musée des Beaux-Arts in Orléans, France. The museum immediately ordered replacement parts from the security company in Luxembourg that had originally installed the system. The company didn't have the parts and ordered them from their supplier in Mumbai. The supplier sent the request to their fabrication facility in Bangalore, which was working at full capacity making a component for Apple's new iPhone, a job that was far more lucrative than making a run of a tiny obscure part for an outdated window alarm sensor. So the part still had not been made. Exactly eighty-seven people were aware of the gap in the museum's security. Eighty-eight, if you counted the Nicolas Fox imposter, who had a friend at the security company.

Twenty-four hours after stealing the Vermeer in Cologne, the imposter arrived in Orléans, toured the museum, and paid very special attention to the window with the broken alarm. Like all of the windows on the ground floor, it had an expanding metal grate on the inside that was secured at night with a simple padlock. There weren't any elaborate interior security systems, like motion detectors or infrared beams, because the galleries were patrolled by armed guards. But the guards couldn't be everywhere at once, and the imposter knew their patrol schedule.

Later that same night, the impersonator took a leisurely stroll in an oversize hoodie down Rue Fernand Rabier, holding what looked like an open can of beer. After pausing in front of the museum's unsecured window to admire the magnificent Cathédrale Saint-Croix, the imposter poured the paint thinner he'd been carrying in the beer can onto the screws of the vertical metal strip that divided and secured the window's two panes of glass.

The imposter returned the following night at 2:00 A.M. He was once again in his hoodie, plus he was wearing rubber gloves and a Nick Fox mask. He carried two cardboard mailing tubes and a shoulder bag containing a battery-operated screwdriver, a box cutter, and a set of lock picks. The paint thinner he'd poured on the mullion the night before had loosened the screws, and he was able to remove them quickly. He detached the mullion and the panes of glass they'd held in place and set them carefully on the street. He picked the padlock, slid open the grate, and slipped inside the museum. The break-in took less than two minutes.

"*Merde alors! Nom d'un chien!* You were right," said Commissaire Killian Bernard of the OCBC, the Office Central de Lutte Contre le Trafic des Biens Culturels, the elite art robbery unit of the French judicial police. He was sitting at a window table beside Kate O'Hare. They were inside the dark Café des Beaux Arts on Rue Dupanloup, across the square from the museum. They both watched the break-in unfold with night-vision binoculars.

The French detective, a big, wide-bodied man of Scottish and French descent, had been skeptical when Kate showed up in his office in Paris two days earlier and insisted that Nicolas Fox would strike the Musée des Beaux-Arts in Orléans within forty-eight hours. Her explanation had been vague, verging on totally evasive. But given the daring thefts Fox had committed in Europe over the past week, and Kate's expertise where this thief was concerned, Bernard couldn't risk ignoring her warning. So he mobilized his team and went to Orléans, a one-hour drive from Paris, and staked out the museum.

Kate was dizzy with relief when the thief appeared on the scene. She'd been tortured with uncertainty ever since she'd arrived in Orléans. There were tons of cities beginning with the letter *O* or *K*. This was the only one she was certain Nick had struck before. He'd broken into this same museum six years ago. But that didn't mean he hadn't committed some con or theft in one of the other possible cities, such as Osaka, Oslo, or Oxford. Not to mention Kansas City, Kathmandu, and Kawasaki.

"How would you like to proceed, Agent O'Hare?" Bernard asked. When he spoke in English, he sounded like Inspector Clouseau trying to imitate Sean Connery. "Shall we move in now, or shall we wait?"

"Let's grab him as he's climbing out the window. It's when he'll be the most vulnerable."

As if on cue, the thief carefully reached out the window and set the cardboard tubes on the sidewalk. The entire theft, from break-in to escape, had taken less than five minutes.

Bernard picked up his radio and gave the command to move. *"On y va! On y va!"*

The thief swung his legs out the window, but before his feet touched the ground, uniformed police officers swarmed around him.

Kate and Bernard emerged from the café and walked across the square as the thief was handcuffed and patted down for weapons. He was smaller than Kate had expected, and at close range the mask was obvious and the effect was chilling. An officer pulled back the hood and removed the mask, and everyone gasped. The thief was a woman.

"*Incroyable,*" Bernard said.

7

The police headquarters, the Hôtel de Police, was a decaying four-story block of concrete that was built quickly and cheaply in the hurried post–World War II reconstruction of Orléans. It had been eroding from neglect ever since.

The interrogation room was like the hundreds of others Kate had been in, right down to the unevenly balanced chair used to keep the suspect on edge. Kate sat across the table from the thief, whose fingerprints had identified her as Serena Blake. She was in her mid-thirties but could have passed for ten years younger. Her brown hair, colored to match Nick's, was styled in a pixie cut that brought out the sharp features of her face, her slender nose and prominent cheekbones. She wore a black tank top that hugged her body like a too-tight leotard. She had the strong, slender physique of a gymnast, which made sense, given what Kate now knew about her. Police records showed that Serena Blake was a British citizen who'd spent two years in prison for burglary in her early twenties and, although she hadn't been arrested since then, was known to be an expert cat burglar. And because Kate had collected extensive information on Nick while she was chasing him, she knew he'd worked with Serena.

"We caught you red-handed stealing a Modigliani and a Degas from a museum," Kate said. "You'll do ten years for that. And when you get out, the Turkish police will be waiting to lock you up in Diyarbakir Prison for God knows how many years. It's so hellish there that prisoners have set themselves on fire rather than endure their sentences. After that, assuming you haven't killed yourself, your time in a Tennessee prison will feel like a vacation."

Serena didn't seem shaken by the grim forecast. She'd probably foreseen that future herself.

"If you're so sure that's it for me, end of story, why are you in here talking?" Serena asked.

"Because I might be able to shave a few years off your sentence if you cooperate."

"The way you tell it, you've already got me dead to rights, so what more do you need?"

"You can tell me where we can find the Matisse, the sultan's goblet, and the Vermeer."

Serena gave a thin smile. "No deal."

The artworks were the only leverage Serena had. That she

wasn't willing to use it when it could do her the most good made Kate curious. What was she saving it for? There was something else at play here, and Kate didn't know what it was. So she decided the best way to reveal what she didn't know was to use what she did know.

"Okay, here's an easier one," Kate said. "What do you want from Nicolas Fox?"

"Nothing," Serena said.

"It's obvious that you're desperate to get his attention. That's why you were wearing a Nick Fox mask and planting his finger-prints at crime scenes."

"*If* I did that, it was because he's a famous thief and I wanted you to chase him instead of me."

Kate decided to bluff and go with a crazy guess. "I might have believed that," she said, "if you hadn't hit Nashville, where you were part of the crew that helped Fox swindle Big Mike Gleaberg, and then Istanbul, where you helped him steal the Topkapi Dagger just to prove that it could be done."

Serena blinked hard, clearly startled that Kate knew about their secret crimes. Kate was startled, too, because it meant that maybe Nick actually *had* stolen the dagger and put it back.

Kate pushed on. "You also went out of your way to irritate Fox by framing him for crimes that were so simple in concept and execution that they'd tarnish his reputation for ingenious crimes. Or maybe you're just not smart enough to pull off any-thing more clever."

"I was clever enough to *allegedly* steal a Matisse, a rare

Turkish antiquity, and a Vermeer in three different countries over the course of a little more than a week. How many thieves do you know who could have done that?"

There was a knock at the door, and Commissaire Bernard stuck his head into the room and gestured for Kate to come out.

"What is it?" she asked, joining Bernard in the hall.

"Her lawyer is here."

"It's not even dawn, and she hasn't made any calls. How did he know that she was here?"

"She might have had a hidden *confédéré* on the street who saw us arrest her and alerted her lawyer. But the fact remains, he's here and we must deal with it. I've put him in a conference room."

Kate followed Bernard down the hall to the room. "Does he speak English?" Kate asked.

Bernard reached for the doorknob. "A bit. His name is Jean-Luc Picard."

Kate sucked in some air at the name of the captain of the starship *Enterprise* on *Star Trek: The Next Generation*. Stay calm, she told herself. Don't punch a hole in the wall or have a high blood pressure attack. Just because it's a name Nick would choose doesn't mean it's Nick. Okay, who was she kidding? She knew it was going to be Nick.

She stepped into the room and stared across the conference table at Nick. He was wearing tortoiseshell glasses balanced on a prosthetic Gérard Depardieu nose that loomed over a thick horseshoe mustache that framed his mouth and went down to his chin. He wore a silk lavaliere scarf tied around his neck, a skinny blue blazer over a zip-up sweater, skinny Japanese denim jeans, and blue suede Derby shoes.

Before Kate could say a word, Nick spoke in a rapid stream of fluent French, dramatizing his points with elaborate, dramatic gestures. Bernard interrupted him with a short comment in French that was the only phrase in the conversation that Kate understood. *"Elle ne parle pas français."*

"Oh, please forgive me," Nick said to her. "I assumed you spoke French. I am Jean-Luc Picard, Mademoiselle Blake's *avocat*. I must insist on speaking to my client at once."

Kate narrowed her eyes at Nick. "Jean-Luc Picard. Why is that name so familiar? Do I know you?"

"I would remember someone so beautiful," Nick said. "Even with your hair pulled into that horse's tail you are a goddess."

"Serena Blake hasn't requested a lawyer," Bernard said.

"She has not been given the opportunity yet," Nick said. "Has she?"

"It's a little early for her to be making calls," Bernard said. "It's nearly dawn."

"I am available to my clients at all hours of the day and night to save them from *obscènes abus d'autorité de la police comme ce qui s'est passé ici ce soir,*" Nick said, then caught himself, taking a deep, calming breath. "*Excusez-moi,* I forget myself when I get outraged."

"The goddess would like to have a word in private with Monsieur Picard," Kate said.

"I don't think that's a good idea," Bernard said. "Something might get lost in translation."

"Oh, don't worry," Kate said. "I'll make sure I am understood."

Bernard reluctantly stepped out, closing the door behind him.

"You lied to me," Kate said to Nick. "You're a big, fat liar. You told me you didn't know of any connection other than you. Liar, liar, liar."

"I suspected Serena, but it was only a suspicion. I didn't want to implicate her until I was sure. She was one of four people involved in those jobs. And any one of those four could have told someone else."

Okay, so he'd told a fib to protect a colleague. Understandable. Especially since lying was second nature to him. And there was the code of honor about snitching. She got all that. Sort of. But things were supposed to be different now. He was on the good team. Sort of.

"Where's the trust?" Kate said. "I thought we'd established trust."

"You trust me?"

"Of course not. You're a career criminal, a con man, and a cheat," she said. "But I thought you at least trusted *me*. I'm dependable, responsible, and I've got sterling character. I wouldn't take advantage of your immunity to arrest someone from your old crew."

"Really?"

"Mostly. I suppose there could be circumstances—"

"Exactly," Nick said. "You are *so* the job."

"And you are *so* irritating."

"I love when you get angry," Nick said. "Your nose gets a cute little wrinkle in it."

"Ugh!"

Kate closed her eyes and took a deep breath. Take a moment, she told herself. Think of something calm. A lake. A kitten sleeping. A puffy cloud drifting overhead. She opened her eyes.

He was grinning. "Feel better?"

She felt her nose to see if it was wrinkled. "If you suspected it was Serena, why did I find her first?"

"You guessed Orléans and I guessed Oxford. I ran into an old friend when I got to Oxford and found out Serena was in Orléans. I was watching a half block away from you when she got arrested."

Yes! Kate thought. She'd outsmarted Nick. Woohoo! Yay! She wanted to do her happy dance, but she restrained herself.

"What job did you do in Oxford?" Kate asked.

"It's where I recruited Serena. After I was thrown out of Harvard for cheating, I relocated to England and apprenticed with Duff MacTaggert. Even back then he was a legendary con man. When I left Duff and went out on my own, Serena was one of the first people I recruited. She had gymnastic skills worthy of Cirque du Soleil, and she had natural cunning."

Kate felt some of the air go out of her celebratory balloon.

There was a quality to his voice that she didn't often hear. Hard to put a name to it, but it told her that Serena was more than just a member of Nick's first crew.

"She must mean a lot to you if you're willing to walk into a police station in that outrageous disguise to see her. It's a miracle you haven't been recognized."

"It's human nature," Nick said. "Context is a huge part of how we process information. This is the last place the police expect to see me, so they don't."

Kate thought that was a load of baloney, but she didn't want her nose to wrinkle so she moved on.

"Okay, now what?" she asked him.

"I want to talk to her. You can make it look real by telling Bernard there's the possibility of a plea bargain."

Kate opened the door and gestured for Bernard to come back in. "I told Picard that we'd make a deal, trim some time off Serena's sentence, if he convinces his client to tell us where she's stashed everything that she's stolen. I can talk the U.S. Justice Department into it. Will you back me on that with the French prosecutor?"

Bernard didn't look too happy about it, but he nodded anyway. "We have her, and we have our paintings back, that's what matters to us. So yes, I think I can talk him into it. I can also have a word with my counterpart in Germany, but I doubt Turkish authorities will be so generous."

"They will if they want their goblet back in pristine condition," Nick said.

"All right, Picard," Kate said. "Let's see what you can do for us."

Bernard opened the door to the interrogation room. "Your lawyer is here to see you," he told Serena.

Nick squeezed past Bernard, whose body filled the doorway, and Serena went wide-eyed with surprise.

"Yes, it is I, Jean-Luc," Nick said. "I'm always here for you."

He went to her and kissed both of her cheeks. Bernard grabbed Nick's shoulder and pulled him back with a stern warning. "*Gardez vos distances, Picard.* You may speak to your client, but you must not touch."

"*Oui, bien sûr, je m'en excuse.*" Nick apologized to him, took a seat across the table from Serena, and looked soulfully into her eyes. "Tell me, what horrors have you endured?"

Bernard groaned and closed the door, leaving the lawyer alone to speak with his client.

"I wouldn't call pulling off a string of international heists the most ideal way to communicate with someone," Nick said to Serena.

"You didn't give me any choice. You completely disappeared after your escape from the courthouse in Los Angeles."

"I'm on the FBI and Interpol's most wanted lists," Nick said. "I didn't think it was a good idea to tweet."

"Since I couldn't find you, I came up with a way to make *you* find *me.*"

He had to admire her for that. At least she'd learned something from him.

"Here I am," he said. "What's so important that you'd risk going to prison in four different countries just to get my attention?"

"Are you familiar with Lester Menendez?"

"A really lovely guy," Nick said. "An international thug who got his start in Colombia, worked his way up in the cocaine and heroin trade by murdering the people he worked for, including his own father and uncles, and taking over their operation. He quickly expanded into the United States and Europe by butchering his competition, literally and with sadistic delight. He got very rich and very fat. He narrowly escaped a raid by the DEA, FBI, and ATF on his New Mexico compound two years ago. Rumor is that he fled to Europe, where he had full-body plastic surgery and killed everybody on the surgical team to protect his new identity."

Serena was rigid while Nick was talking. Her lips were pressed tight, her jaw clenched, her eyes steely and unblinking.

"The rumors are true," Serena said. "The bodies of the plastic surgeon and his two assistants were found stuffed into an oil drum off a highway in Spain. Their throats were slit so deeply, they were nearly decapitated. But before they were killed, they were tortured, probably to find out if they'd shared details about Menendez's new identity with anyone else. The plastic surgeon was Sean."

Nick took a moment to absorb the shock. "I'm sorry," he said. "I had no idea."

"It wasn't made public. Sean was quietly buried in the family plot. His obituary said he'd had a short illness."

Nick had never met Serena's older brother, but he knew all about him. Sean was a hardworking, straight-arrow, responsible young man who'd graduated from Oxford University Medical School, married a nice girl, and never had so much as a speeding ticket. Serena, on the other hand, had graduated from Oxford with a bachelor's degree in fine art and started breaking into estates, galleries, and museums.

"Why did Sean agree to operate on Menendez?" Nick asked.

"Sean had big gambling debts. He was about to lose his practice, his wife, his house, everything. He was embarrassed to ask the family for help. The loan sharks put Menendez on to him. I suppose Sean thought the operation would get him out of the hole he'd dug for himself. Instead, he dug himself a grave." She shook her head. "The two of us had it all. We came from a wealthy Oxford family, we had Oxford University educations, and what happened to us? He became a compulsive gambler who got himself killed, and I became a thief who will probably die in prison."

"How can I help?" Nick asked.

"I want to find Menendez and destroy him, but I don't have the skills to do it. You do."

"I'm not an assassin."

"I don't want you to kill him. I want you to take him down. Gut his empire. Empty his bank accounts. Reduce him to nothing. For Menendez, that would be even worse than death. And I want to help you do it, so you'll have to break me out of jail, too."

"I'll do what I can to take down Menendez, but I'm temporarily leaving you behind bars. I don't want to raise any red flags that might spook Menendez."

More than that, he couldn't take a chance on Serena tagging along and discovering he was working for the FBI.

8

Kate and Bernard were in the conference room having an early breakfast of French bread and butter and a few slices of aged ham when Nick knocked once on the doorjamb and stepped in.

"Do we have an agreement?" Kate asked Nick. "Will she tell us where to find the stolen property?"

"Not until she has written assurance from the United States, German, and Turkish authorities that her sentences will be reduced," Nick said.

"That could take weeks," Bernard said.

"She's not going anywhere, no?" Nick said. "We can wait. But the same can't be said for the things you want. The paintings must be kept in climate-controlled conditions, away from moisture and heat. Who knows if they are?"

"She does," Bernard said.

Nick shrugged. "I'd move quickly if I were you, just to be on the safe side. *A bientôt.*"

"*Casse-toi,*" Bernard muttered when Nick left the room. "*Débile.*"

Kate didn't need to speak French to know a profanity and insult when she heard one.

"That goes double for me," she said, earning a smile from Bernard.

Kate returned to her room at the Ibis Orléans Centre Gare, a modern three-star hotel directly across from the train station with the charm of a budget chain in the States. She'd been looking forward to a moment of calm to reorganize, but she'd walked in to the sound of the shower running and Nick's fake mustache lying on the bed like a tiny dead hairy animal.

"*Débile!*" she yelled in the vicinity of the bathroom.

There was no answer so she kicked off her shoes, stretched out on the bed, and put the pillow over her face. She heard the water stop running, then sensed she wasn't alone.

"You're going to miss the good stuff with that pillow over your face," Nick said.

"What good stuff did you have in mind?" she asked.

"Me naked."

Kate took the pillow off her face and looked at him. He was wearing a towel that hung low on his hips.

"You're not naked," Kate said.

"I could be."

She pulled the pillow back over her face.

"I get the feeling you're not happy to see me," Nick said.

"Gee, how'd you figure that one out?"

"I can't hear you," Nick said. "You're talking into the pillow."

Kate ripped the pillow off her face and sat up, pop-eyed, arms flailing. "You have to stop breaking into my room! I need privacy sometimes. I need to get away from you. We're partners, not lovers."

"Your loss," Nick said.

He dropped his towel and stepped into boxer briefs.

"Good grief," Kate said.

Wow! She thought. The man was freaking perfect.

"It turns out that Serena's brother was the plastic surgeon who gave Lester Menendez a new face and a new body," Nick said. "When the operation was complete, Menendez tortured and killed Serena's brother."

"Oh my gosh, how horrible."

"A few years back, a con to trick a Somali warlord out of a piracy ransom went very wrong, and I found myself locked in a tiger cage, facing a sunrise execution. Instead of cutting and running with the rest of my crew, Serena stayed behind, crept into the heavily guarded compound in the middle of the night, and rescued me. We barely made it out of Somalia alive."

"So you owe her."

"Big-time. Even if I didn't, I would still help her. She's a good person, and Menendez is evil."

"She wants you to kill him?"

"No. She wants me to destroy him."

"Nice. I like it."

"I imagine your boss will also like it," Nick said.

"Every law enforcement agency in the world wants Menendez. He still controls a big chunk of the drug trade in North America and Europe. Unfortunately, no one knows what he looks like now or where he is. And even if we did, we don't have his DNA or any fingerprints we can use to identify him. He set fire to his house, so we lost our chance to collect anything we could use to create a DNA profile. And I can guarantee you he also burned off his fingerprints. He could be anybody."

"He's still the same person inside," Nick said. "He still has the same strengths, weaknesses, longings, and obsessions. Before his radical surgery, Menendez was a fat man who put on the pounds devouring the most expensive and rare chocolates in the world. I can guarantee he still likes them. He's also been obsessed with finding sunken treasure ever since he was a kid in Colombia and found doubloons that washed ashore from a seventeenth-century shipwreck. Those are the weaknesses we're going to exploit."

"You think you can just wave a Hershey bar and some gold coins under the right nose, and he'll introduce himself to you?"

"Pretty much. I came up with something in the shower."

The image of Nick naked was burned into Kate's brain, and she had a vision of what else came up in the shower.

"We're going to use Menendez's lust for rare chocolate to narrow down his new identity," Nick said. "Once we've found him, we're going to convince him that we've discovered the legendary *Santa Isabel,* a Spanish galleon that sank in a storm in 1502 off the coast of Portugal with over a billion dollars' worth of treasure on board."

"That's the bait," she said. "What's the trap?"

"I'm still refining some of the details on the trap."

"Oh boy," Kate said. "You don't know the details."

"I know some of them." He flipped the quilt back and sat on the edge of the bed.

Kate's eyes got wide. "What are you doing?"

"Going to bed. I've been up all night."

"This is *my* bed."

"It's *our* bed."

"No, no, no. There's no *our.* Get out of my bed," Kate said.

"No."

"I could shoot you, you know. I'm an FBI agent and you're a felon."

"You don't have a gun."

Damn. He was right. She hated not having a gun. And she missed her FBI windbreaker. This whole out-of-country thing sucked.

"What about the trap details?" she asked him. "Don't you want to work out the details?"

"I know we want to recruit your dad, and probably the crew we've used in the past. Tom Underhill, Willie, and Boyd Capwell. I'll work out the rest of the details while I sleep." He slipped under the quilt and patted the spot next to him. "Come to bed and leave it all to me. I do some of my best work when I'm in bed."

Kate was sure that was true.

Jake O'Hare approached his Denny's Grand Slam breakfast like one of the many covert military operations he'd led for Uncle Sam before his retirement. He nibbled at it from various angles, picking away at the egg whites until the yolk was completely exposed, conquering the yolk with some strategic stabs of bacon, then attacking the unprotected mountain of buttermilk pancakes in a full frontal assault that didn't leave a surviving crumb. When he was done, he carefully mopped everything up with his toast until the plate was clean and there was no evidence he'd ever touched it.

Kate had just come back to L.A. on a red-eye from Paris, and had cleaned her plate with a lot less cunning than her dad.

"I love watching you eat, Dad," Kate said. "You're so methodical about it."

Jake took a sip of his coffee, black with no sugar, and leaned back in the booth, resting a tan, muscled arm on the top of the vinyl seat. He kept his body in lean fighting shape and his gray hair trimmed in a regulation buzz cut, more out of habit than anything else.

"I'm methodical about everything," Jake said. "And I'm cute. Yesterday I was in the supermarket and the checkout lady told me I was adorable."

"Kittens and baby shoes are adorable," Kate said. "Do you really want to be lumped together with kittens and baby shoes?"

"I was in the ten-items-or-less line with twelve items and she didn't kick me out. Adorable can have its benefits."

Kate leaned forward and lowered her voice. "Is your passport current?"

"I'm sure one of 'em is," he said. "Who would you like me to kidnap?"

"Nobody. And you can't say things like that around me in public. I'm an officer of the law, remember?"

"Sorry, I should have said 'apprehend by extraordinary rendition.' There's nothing illegal about that. At least that was what I was told by the CIA when I was grabbing suspected terrorists out of their beds in one country and dragging them to a secret prison in another." He accepted more coffee from the waitress. "Those were good times. How about regime change? Would you like a dictator toppled?"

"Close. I need to take down the drug lord of a global narcotics empire. It's a rogue operation. We'll be on foreign soil without any backup, going up against a sadist and his army of trained killers."

"Just another day at the office."

And almost a decade ago, that had been a typical day for him. But that was before he collected his military pension and moved in with Kate's younger sister, Megan, her accountant husband, and their two kids. The home was in Calabasas, California, just a few miles away from the Denny's where they were eating. Now most of his battles were waged on the golf course, except when Kate occasionally asked for his help. Jake was the only one besides Bolton and Jessup who knew the truth about her and Nick . . . and the only one she could entirely trust.

"Does your boss at the FBI know about this?" Jake asked.

"I called Jessup from the airport and filled him in. He's completely on board. It was an easy sell. This is exactly the kind of high-profile criminal that Deputy Director Bolton and Jessup broke Nick out of jail to catch. I'm going to stop by the office for a more detailed briefing when I leave here."

"I assume you're going to assemble a team."

"We're going to recruit Tom, Willie, and Boyd," she said. "You've met them on past operations. Nick also has a tech guy in mind. And we're going to need you and a couple of your buddies with naval experience. Specifically, a chief engineer to handle everything down below and a boatswain to handle everything on deck. We'll pay top dollar."

He shook his head. "You'll only have to pay their expenses. The guys I have in mind will do the job just for fun."

"They could get killed."

"That's the fun part. And it beats the hell out of dying of boredom."

She studied her father. "Is that why you're helping me? Are you that miserable not being in the field anymore?"

"Of course not. I love living with Megan, Roger, and the grandkids. It's the family life I never got to have when you and your sister were growing up. And when Megan and Roger aren't around, I get to teach the kids important life skills."

"Like how to make explosives out of household cleaning supplies."

"They're way past that now," he said.

"They're five and seven years old."

"They're fast learners. Now we're working on how to kill a man with whatever you've got handy in your sack lunch. Do you remember when you used to practice that?"

"Yeah, you taught me how to smother a man with a sandwich baggie, and how to shove a straw up his nose into his brain. Those are treasured memories. I think of you every time I eat a sandwich."

"A father can't ask for more than that."

"So if you enjoy retirement so much, why leave Tyler and Sara and go off and risk your life with me?"

"There are still a few things I can teach you," he said. "For instance, do you know how to make a field battery?"

"A *what*?"

"A battery made out of potatoes, copper wire, and a few nails."

"Nope," she said, though she couldn't imagine a situation where she'd need one.

"There you go," he said. "Besides, there's nobody who is going to watch your back better than me. You know that."

"That's why I'm here."

"And that's why I'm going to be there with you, wherever

there is, any time you ask and as long as I'm able," he said. "It's what fathers do."

"Most fathers don't show up with hand grenades and bowie knives."

"They should be ashamed of themselves," Jake said.

9

The Caterpillar 797F mining dump truck was twenty-four feet tall, forty-nine feet long, thirty-two feet wide, and rolled on six tires that were each thirteen feet high and five feet wide. The sticker price of a 797F, with cup holders, was $5.5 million. It wasn't a sporty drive. It was like driving a two-story building, as Wilma "Willie" Owens discovered for herself as she tried to steer the massive vehicle through the barren landscape outside the Black Butte open-pit coal mine. Willie had already flattened a mine supervisor's unoccupied car like a beer can and was heading straight for an office trailer, sending the lone watch-man scrambling out the door in terror.

Willie might have had an easier time controlling the truck if she'd logged the weeks of training in a simulator that a 797F driver is required to do. Instead, she'd put on a pair of skinny jeans, squeezed into a tank top that barely held her double-Ds, and sashayed into the Mint Bar in Sheridan, Wyoming, where the dump truck drivers from the mine hung out. Willie had an insatiable desire and natural ability to drive anything with a motor on land, sea, or air. Problem was, she was entirely self-taught, and almost always unlicensed, which meant there could be a steep, and destructive, learning curve.

Willie was wandering around her early fifties, but in the dim light of the bar she'd looked twenty years younger, and her bleached blond hair looked pretty darn sexy. The effect was enhanced by the copious amounts of alcohol that was consumed by the bar's patrons.

Buck Breznick was a dump truck driver who'd had two pitchers of beer and enough whiskey shots to think it was a good idea to take Willie out to see his massive truck in the middle of the night.

"Buck, honey," Willie said, looking up at the 797F, pressing her breast into his arm, "I'd do just about anything to get into the cab of this big boy."

The mine was closed and deserted and Buck thought "Just about anything" sounded like exactly what he needed, so they crept up the metal staircase that was across the front of the 797F's massive two-story grill, and into the operator's cab. They spent a few hours messing around before falling asleep.

When dawn broke, Willie slipped into the driver's seat, fired up the 4,000 hp engine, and pressed the pedal to the floor. Buck was still passed out in the passenger seat, which was probably a blessing, considering the learning curve for driving the truck was steeper than Willie'd anticipated.

She stomped on the brakes just before rolling over the car, but the beast didn't exactly stop on a dime. It continued on course and smashed through the office trailer in an explosion of corrugated metal, glass, and thousands of pieces of paper.

Willie finally brought the truck to a stop, blew a kiss to Buck, who was snoring away, and snatched her high heels off the floor. She made her way down the stairs, holding her high heels in her hands as if she were leaving an apartment after an all-night party and not fleeing the cab of one of the largest vehicles on earth. By the time she got to the bottom step, two private security vehicles had screeched up, and four uniformed officers were waiting for her. They all looked at her in shocked silence, like she was some kind of alien emerging from her flying saucer.

Willie tossed the dump truck keys to one of the astonished guards. "You park it, honey. But don't scratch the paint."

"You're under arrest," another guard said, holding a pair of handcuffs.

His hands were shaking, which made Willie smile as she sat down on the step and slipped on her high heels. He was in his twenties and filled out his uniform nicely.

"I bet you'll enjoy putting those cuffs on me," she said. "Bet you'd enjoy it even more if you let me put them on you sometime."

A dark Chevy Impala slid to a stop in a cloud of dust. A

man emerged from the car in a dark suit and wearing dark sunglasses. The crowd parted for the stranger, who quickly flipped open a leather case and flashed a badge of some kind, then slapped it shut and stuck it back in his pocket.

"John Doggett, FBI," Nick Fox said. "I'll take over from here."

"You know her?" the guard with the cuffs asked.

"Sydney Bristow. She's wanted in seventeen states for vehicular mayhem."

"I didn't know that was a federal offense," Willie said.

"It is when you do it in seventeen states," Nick said, taking her by the arm and leading her to his car. "You're in big trouble, Sydney."

"It was a big truck," she said.

"You have the right to remain silent. I suggest you use it." He put her into the backseat of the car, slammed the door, and turned back to the guards. "Tell your bosses they'll find her at the federal courthouse in Casper."

Nick got into the car, backed up, and sped off before the guards could think any more about it. He glanced in the rear-view mirror at Willie, and she winked at him.

"My hero," Willie said.

She didn't know Nick's full name, but he was hotter than a stolen Ferrari and just as fast, sleek, and dangerous. Over the last year or so, he'd hired her a few times to drive a variety of cars, boats, and planes in several big cons to bring down bad guys for some shadowy firm called Intertect. It was fishy, and very illegal, but she liked adventure. And she liked him.

"What would you have done if I hadn't shown up?" Nick asked.

"I'd have been arrested. So I would've flirted with the cops for a few hours, posted bail, gone back to my hotel with that young security guard and had some fun, and then skedaddled out of the state and skipped the trial."

"Is that what you do with all the money we pay you? Use it to jump bail when you take joyrides in stolen cars?"

"That wasn't just any car, honey, it's the biggest one on earth. Now I can tick that off my bucket list."

"What else would you like to drive?"

"A bullet train. An Apache attack helicopter. The Hennessey Venom GT. The stealth bomber."

"How about a hundred-and-fifty-foot cargo ship?"

"That doesn't sound very sexy."

"Did I mention it's in Portugal, and we'll pay you a hundred thousand dollars?"

"Deal," she said.

"Don't you want to know who our target is?"

"Not really. But I am curious what that piece of tin was that you flashed to those security guards back there."

He reached into his pocket and tossed the leather case into the backseat. She caught it and opened it up. It was a Geek Squad badge from Best Buy.

"Remind me never to play poker with you," she said. "You're too good at bluffing."

. . .

The talk show set in the Simi Valley, California, soundstage looked like every other one on late-night television. There was a desk, a chair, and a couch lined up against a backdrop of the Hollywood Hills. But this was no Jimmy Fallon, Conan, or David Letterman show. This studio audience was paid to attend and the host wasn't a comedian but, rather, an actor, Boyd Capwell, hired to play the part. Boyd was perfectly cast for the role. He was good-looking in an aging anchorman sort of way, had a full head of hair, great teeth, and wore a suit well.

"Welcome back to *Straight Talk*. My guest tonight is Delmer Pratt of Beaumont, Texas," Boyd said, staring into the camera. "His life was spiraling into madness and despair until he discovered Uberboner, the incredible herbal remedy for impotence."

The audience applauded. Delmer sat stiffly in his chair and nodded his thanks. He wore a John Deere cap, flannel shirt, jeans, and work boots. He was a real Uberboner user, but he'd been given the clothes to wear, a script to learn, and a check to make his humiliation worthwhile.

"For years, I carried a secret shame. I wasn't able to satisfy my wife's womanly needs the way a husband should." Delmer repeated his lines in the unnatural tone of someone not used to reciting memorized dialogue. "I was slow, soft, and listless, unable to stand at attention in the bedroom. I needed to man up before my marriage and my self-respect completely crumbled. Fortunately for me, one of my friends recommended Uberboner, the affordable herbal remedy available only on TV.

Now I am ten times the man I ever was, and my marriage has been saved."

"That's truly amazing, Delmer, and I'm happy for you and your wife," Boyd said. "But now that you're manly again, have you ever wondered what caused the problem in the first place?"

"Excuse me?" Delmer asked.

It was the first thing he'd said that wasn't scripted and memorized.

Boyd leaned toward him earnestly. "What was your relationship with your mother like?"

"My mother?" Delmer looked to someone offstage. "What the hell does my mother have to do with this?"

"Impotence is often more psychological than physical," Boyd said. "You've solved the blood-flow problem, but what about what's happening in your head?"

"Who gives a crap about that?"

"You will when the pill stops working and you become a limp noodle again, because your inner demons come roaring back to life."

"CUT!"

A gray-haired man in a doctor's lab coat marched onto the set and up to Boyd's desk. He was Dr. Landry, the inventor of Uberboner. He was also the writer, director, financier of the infomercial, and the next scheduled guest.

"What kind of question was that?" Landry asked Boyd.

"The obvious one," Boyd said. "I'm trying to get the whole story."

"The only story is what's in the script," Landry said.

"I have journalistic integrity."

"You're an actor."

"My *character* has journalistic integrity," Boyd said.

"No, he doesn't. He has no integrity of any kind. He exists to sell my pills."

"You know nothing about him."

"I wrote the script," Landry said.

"But you didn't develop the character at all. I had to fill in all the blanks. Did you know his father was a war correspondent who died in Vietnam? That's where he got his passion for journalism and pursuing the truth in every story."

"This is an infomercial," Landry said. "A long commercial, understand? It's not a drama."

"You want this to look like a real talk show, right? You want people to believe they are getting actual news," Boyd said. "To do that, my character has to be authentic."

"Your character has to repeat the lines in the script exactly as written," Landry said. "Or your character will be an unemployed actor."

Boyd's phone vibrated in his pocket. He took it out and answered it.

"It's me," Kate said. "Did I call at a bad time?"

Boyd recognized her voice instantly. It was the mysterious agent for an even more mysterious security firm that used cons to bring down big-time criminals. She and her partner, Nick, had given him the best, and most lucrative, roles of his career, even if it was always for an audience of one, who usually ended up in prison.

"You have impeccable timing, as usual," Boyd said. "I'm in."

"You don't even know what the job is, what the risks are, or what we're paying."

"What's my role?"

"You'll be the captain of a research vessel on the high seas."

"Captain Phillips meets Horatio Hornblower," he said.

"If you say so."

"You know I'd do anything for you, Woody."

"Woody?" Kate asked.

"I'm on my way," Boyd said, ending the call.

"What do you mean, you're 'on your way'?" Dr. Landry said. "We're still shooting. We aren't finished yet."

"Sorry, but Woody Allen needs me in New York for a part. You of all people should appreciate that I can't ignore a Woody emergency." Boyd smiled at his own wit, took a bow, and walked off the set.

A flying saucer from an alien world had crashed into a tree in the backyard of a tract home in Newport Beach, California. The silver spacecraft, scorched from its fiery descent through the earth's atmosphere, was lodged precariously in the tree's branches. An escape ladder ran down along the tree trunk to a perfectly manicured lawn where a dozen excited six-year-olds were lined up to get inside the saucer. At the head of the line, scrambling up the ladder, was deliriously happy Bobby Nickerson, Jr., who still had birthday cake all over his face and couldn't wait to get into his Best Birthday Present Ever.

"Freaking amazing," said Bobby, Sr., admiring his son's flying saucer. "It's the treehouse to end all treehouses."

"I hope not, or I'm out of business," said Tom Underhill, who'd spent the past six weeks building it.

It was thanks to innovative treehouses like the flying saucer that Tom was written up as one of Southern California's visionary entrepreneurs. Problem was, not many people could afford a $50,000 indulgence for their kids. He certainly couldn't for his two kids. The treehouse he'd built for them was pretty basic. The only special feature was a fireman's pole for a quick escape.

Bobby, Sr., shook Tom's hand, thanked him again, and then cut to the front of the line to climb up into the treehouse himself.

Tom stayed for a while and watched everyone enjoy his creation. He had cake and ice cream. He took a couple balloons for his kids, waved goodbye to the Nickersons, and showed himself out of the backyard. He reached the street where he'd parked his pickup and was surprised to see Nick.

"Now you're going to have to come back next year and build Hogwarts for that kid," Nick said to Tom.

"That's my fiendish plot," Tom said with a grin, thinking if anybody knew about fiendish plotting, it was Nick. A year or so ago, Nick had come along out of nowhere and saved Tom's house from foreclosure. In return, Tom had helped Nick transform a derelict Palm Springs McMansion into a Mexican drug lord's fortified compound. It was part of an outrageous con to trick a sleazy Beverly Hills lawyer into revealing where his fugitive client was hiding. It was the most fun Tom had ever had.

"I could use your help on a new job," Nick said.

"I was hoping you'd say that."

"How would you like to go to Portugal, transform a cargo boat into a research vessel, and build me a remotely operated deep-sea submersible rover with cameras, lights, and claws, and the high-tech command center that runs it?"

"I would," Tom said. "But I don't know anything about building a robotic sub."

"It doesn't have to work," Nick said. "It only has to look amazing."

"That I can do," Tom said, already feeling a shot of adrenaline hitting his bloodstream. He could tell his wife he'd been hired to build a treehouse in Portugal for some rich guy. He'd learned from Nick that the best lies were the ones that were substantially truthful. She wouldn't argue if the money was right and he wasn't away too long, because the money wasn't exactly flowing in from the treehouse business.

"I take it we're tricking another very bad man," Tom said.

"The worst," Nick said. "We're taking down a sadistic monster."

"Is what we're doing illegal?"

"As far as I know, I don't think there are any laws against

tricking a killer into being captured by law enforcement. But I wouldn't put it on your résumé."

"When do you need me?"

"Right away. You'll have three weeks to build everything and we'll pay you a hundred thousand dollars. Tax free."

"Now, that *is* illegal."

"I won't tell anyone if you won't," Nick said.

10

The $150 million 3-D movie version of the 1970s TV series *The Man from Atlantis* starred an unknown Australian actor as a water-breathing man who washes up on Santa Monica beach after an earthquake in the Pacific. He becomes a secret agent for the United States government, and in his quest to find the lost city of Atlantis, the fish with a license to kill stops a super-villain from destroying the world with his earthquake-making machine.

Critics loathed the movie, but it grossed nearly $400 million at the box office, and it won an Academy Award for its incredible computer-generated underwater effects, designed by Rodney Smoot and his team at Magical Realism VFX.

Unfortunately, the Oscar wasn't enough to keep Magical Realism afloat. Rodney had sunk every penny he had into the company, but it became a casualty of outsourcing, and Rodney was bankrupted. He'd pink-slipped all his employees, and the bank was about to foreclose on his vast Santa Monica warehouse. Rodney was in the warehouse in the process of removing a poster from his office wall when he was startled to see a man and a woman standing outside his door.

"The bankruptcy auction isn't until next Saturday," Rodney said.

"How much would it take to call off the auction, get the bank off your back, and allow you to keep all of this?" Nick asked with a sweep of his arm.

"Five million dollars," Rodney said.

Nick looked at Kate. "I think we can swing that, don't you?"

"It's pricey," she said. "But yes, we can."

Nick smiled and turned back to Rodney. "There you go. You're back in business."

Rodney stared at them, bewildered. "I don't understand."

"We want you to create some visual effects for us," Nick said. "Specifically, an underwater debris field from a Spanish treasure galleon that sank five hundred years ago. Our underwater footage needs to be interactive, allowing the viewer to go wherever he wants."

"So you want me to do the effects for a game," Rodney said.

"A *con* game," Kate said. "By creating these effects, you'll be helping us capture a fugitive drug lord who has killed a lot of people."

"Are you with the government?" Rodney asked.

"We're with a private security firm," Kate said. "It's important that you understand that we aren't authorized by any government or law enforcement agency to do what we have in mind."

"But it's for the greater good," Nick said. "And you could also put a lot of the people that you fired back to work."

"What exactly do you need me to do?" Rodney asked.

"Create what the camera on a remotely operated underwater vehicle would see on the ocean floor," Nick said. "We'll be watching the feed on monitors in the control room of a salvage vessel and controlling the rover's camera, and robotic arms, with a joystick. We'll be picking up some treasure and bringing it back up, so we've got to see that, too."

"Let me see if I've got this straight," Rodney said. "We'll be free-roaming through a photo-realistic CGI environment, but all you need to see on your monitor is whatever is within the view of the camera on this rover, nothing else."

"That's right," Nick said.

"So you'll only be able to see what the rover's lights illuminate in the murk, and the image only has to be good enough for crappy video resolution," Rodney said, clearly warming to the challenge. "That makes things a lot easier. It'll take at least six weeks to create the effects."

"You have three," Nick said.

"Geez, you're no better than a movie studio. Paying off the bank for the equipment and debt will only be the beginning of the costs," Rodney said. "We'll need to hire about forty people. Code writers. Modelers. Texture artists. Lighting specialists. What'll we tell them that they are working on?"

"A demo for a big investor who's interested in a new role-playing game," Nick said. "We'll have them sign intimidating nondisclosure agreements, so they can't say anything about their work without forfeiting their salaries and facing a terrifying lawsuit."

"Will that NDA protect them from getting arrested with me if this all goes to hell?" Rodney asked.

"Yep," Kate said. "It will prove they are innocent dupes who didn't have any idea what they were actually working on."

"All right, then," Rodney nodded, satisfied with her answer. "We've got the code to create the water effect, the ocean floor, and the aquatic life from our work on *The Man from Atlantis*. That's a huge head start, but we're still going to have to create the lighting effects and build the objects that are illuminated in the debris field and the parts of the rover, like the robot arm, that we'll see from the camera. That will cost about five to seven hundred thousand dollars, but then you're going to need a render farm on your boat."

"What's a render farm?" Nick asked.

"Basically fifty computers strung together to create a supercomputer capable of generating the interactive virtual world in real time," Rodney said. "The good news is, you can buy the whole shebang pre-built in a shipping container, with cooling systems and everything, and have it delivered to your door wherever you are. There are a bunch of companies that do it. Figure another two hundred and fifty thousand for that."

"We'll need you on the boat with us, to run the show and make sure nothing goes wrong," Kate said. "The drug lord we're going after is a sadistic killer. If he discovers he's being conned, he won't hesitate to have his men butcher all of us in the most gruesome and painful way possible."

"In other words," Rodney said, "my life, and yours, could depend on how convincing my special effects are."

"Yes, that's right," Kate said.

Rodney grinned. "Cool! How could a true special effects artist possibly resist a challenge like that?"

On a sunny Saturday afternoon, Kate and Jake met Nick on the yacht in Marina del Rey to go over the fine points of the plan. Nick had set out a mountain of taco salad, a selection of cigars, and an ice-filled tub stocked with beer.

"I've found a hundred-and-fifty-foot cargo carrier in a boatyard in Lisbon," Jake said, relaxing on the flybridge, a beer in one hand and a half-smoked Cohiba Behike in the other. "It was built in the 1980s and is currently registered in Sierra Leone, where there's only one safety regulation I know of, and it's more of a suggestion, really. They like the boat to be able to float. But no worries, it's been refurbished from top to bottom. She has a working crane for the sub, a cargo hold big enough for your container full of computers, is loaded with all the latest electronics, and can hit a top speed of ten knots. It's a steal at six hundred thousand dollars."

"What's the catch?" Kate asked.

"It's literally a steal," Jake said. "But nobody is looking for it anymore. The ship was hijacked in the South China Sea twenty years ago and has been repainted, renamed, and reflagged at least a dozen times since. I've dealt with this ship broker before on plenty of covert jobs. His word is good. We can leave the boat at the backwater wharf where it's docked now while Tom does the remodel and builds the sub. Nobody will bother us there."

"Perfect," Nick said. "Go to Lisbon and make the deal. There's a million dollars waiting for you in Barnaby Jones's bank account at Barclays."

"Who is Barnaby Jones?" Jake asked.

"You are," Nick said. "I have a fake passport and credit cards for you in Barnaby's name."

"I like the way you operate."

"Likewise," Nick said.

Kate inwardly groaned and reached for corn chips. Their little bromance would have been unbearable if not for the food and beer.

"I'll leave in two days," Jake said. "I'd go sooner, but I've got my colonoscopy tomorrow, and at my age, you want to be sure there's nothing in the chimney but soot."

"I'd keep that information on a need-to-know basis," Kate said. "And believe me, there's nobody who does. I wish I didn't."

"Tom will fly out with you," Nick said. "He's never been overseas before, so you'll have to hold his hand."

"We have a movie tech genius," Kate said to Jake. "His name is Rodney Smoot, and he'll show up after his team in L.A. is done creating the effects. He'll set up his render farm in the cargo hold. It will be up to you and your guys to get Tom and Rodney whatever materials they need and keep them both out of trouble while they work."

"I've babysat dictators and defectors," Jake said. "I think I can handle a treehouse builder and a guy who makes movies."

"Who have you recruited to help out?" Kate asked.

"On deck, I've got Lou Ould-Abdallah, an ex–Somali pirate who did a few black ops jobs with me in the South China Sea. He goes by Billy Dee Snipes now."

"'Billy Dee Snipes'?" Kate said. "What kind of name is that?"

"One that's easier to pronounce than Lou Ould-Abdallah," Jake said. "He lives in a seniors-only condo complex in Las Vegas now and hangs out at Treasure Island Casino playing slots to remind himself of the good old days. For down below, I've got Barnacle Bob Baker, the best engineer on the high seas. He's spent so much time in engine rooms that he can't abide fresh air and sunshine. His hands only feel clean to him when they're covered in grease and grime. Bob has been working on the ferry that runs between Dover and Calais because he needs to be in an engine room at sea. The monotony and the lack of risk is grinding him down. He'll gladly do this just for the change of scenery." Jake took a long drag on his cigar and let the smoke slowly curl out of his mouth. "If you're going to convince a drug lord as smart, vicious, and untrusting as Lester Menendez that you've found sunken treasure, it's going to take more than a survey boat, a robot sub, and some pretty pictures. The greedy bastard will want to take some coins off the ocean floor himself."

"Of course he will," Nick said.

"The coins can't be all nice and shiny, either," Jake said. "They'll have to be caked in hard sediment like they've been down there for centuries."

"That's true," Nick said.

"Where are you going to get coins like that?"

"We're going to steal them."

"That's what I figured, knowing you," Jake said. "But you're taking a huge gamble with my daughter's life that Menendez isn't going to hear about the theft, recognize the stolen goods, and shoot you both in the face."

"He's more likely to cut off our limbs with a chainsaw," Kate said. "And stuff us into an oil drum filled with acid."

"I'd like to avoid that," Nick said. "That's why we're going to steal some sunken treasure still covered with schmutz without anyone noticing it's gone."

"Do you know where and how you're going to do that?"

"I do."

Jake grinned, nodded to himself, and glanced over at Kate. "How did you ever catch this guy?"

"I conned him," she said.

Nick relaxed back into his chair and studied Kate. He'd underestimated her when she was chasing him. Not something he'd ever do again. He'd known she was smart and tenacious. He hadn't counted on her being devious as well. And he hadn't anticipated the intensity of the attraction he felt for her.

"She's devious," Nick said. "It's her best quality. It's one of the few things we have in common."

Jake reached for another cold beer. "She gets that from me."

"I'm not devious," Kate said. "I'm diligent and determined in my pursuit of justice."

"There's still one crucial aspect of this scheme that neither of you have talked about," Jake said. "How you're going to find Lester Menendez, a fugitive who has a new face, a new body, a new name, no fingerprints on file, and could be anywhere on earth. No law enforcement agencies have been able to find him."

"That's because they've been chasing Menendez instead of making him come to them," Kate said.

"I don't see how you can make Menendez come to you," Jake said.

"It's how I was caught," Nick said, smiling at Kate, toasting her with his beer bottle.

11

In 1807 the *Nuestra Señora de Santa Maria,* laden with fifteen tons of gold from South America, was on its way back to Spain when it sank in a fierce storm off the coast of Portugal. More than two hundred years later, a UK-based treasure hunting company, Global Marine Ventures, found the wreckage. They quietly salvaged five hundred thousand gold coins, worth a half billion dollars, over the course of three weeks. They didn't announce their find until they'd taken the coins back to London in thousands of sealed plastic buckets full of water for preservation.

The Spanish government took the treasure hunters to court in the UK, claiming the coins were valuable cultural artifacts that belonged to Spain and had been stolen from the ocean floor. Global Marine Ventures argued that the sunken ship was in international waters outside of any country's jurisdiction and that the treasure was fair game for anyone who found it.

The case stretched on for years, but the court ultimately agreed with Spain, and not only awarded the Spanish government all of the plunder, but also reimbursement of their legal costs, plus interest. The judgment sank Global Marine Ventures. The buckets of coins, still encrusted in sediment, were flown to the National Museum of Underwater Archeology in Cartagena, Spain, for restoration and eventual display.

Three months after the delivery of the coins to Spain, and five days after Nick, Kate, and Jake met on the yacht in Marina del Rey, Nick and Kate stood sipping coffee on the veranda of Nick's south-facing fifth-floor suite at the NH Cartagena Hotel. Nick had been in the city for several days preparing for the theft of the coins. Kate had just arrived.

"Nice view," Kate said, looking out at the harbor and the museum, a sleek atrium of stone, glass, and sharp angles.

Their hotel was on the edge of the old town, just north of the sea wall and the Paseo Alfonso XII roadway that went along the waterfront. Down below and straight ahead was a wide plaza and wharf leading to the cruise ship terminal, where an ocean liner was docked. The museum was on the east side of the plaza. A small shopping center and the yacht marina were to the west. Further south, Kate could see a lighthouse at the edge of the bay and, beyond that, the sun glistening off the swells of the Mediterranean.

Nick gestured to the museum. "That's where our gold is.

What you're seeing is basically a large skylight. The bulk of the museum is underground to give the visitors the sensation of going underwater. That's a plus for us."

"How do you figure that?"

"The broad plaza between the museum to the east, the cruise ship dock to the south, and the shopping center to the west is a multilevel underground parking garage. The thing about underground garages is that they need lots of ventilation to prevent people from dying of carbon monoxide poisoning. They pump a lot of air in and out. So does the museum, because it's almost entirely underground and there wouldn't be enough fresh air circulating otherwise. The two networks of large air ducts run alongside each other to the surface."

She could see where this line of thought was going. "We're going to break into the museum tonight through the air ducts in the garage."

"This afternoon," Nick said.

Kate stared at him. "In broad daylight?"

"It's the best way not to be noticed when we're breaking in and leaving. There are people everywhere."

"Not in the conservation lab grabbing handfuls of coins."

"You'll just have to make sure you're not seen."

"Me? Where are you going to be?"

"I'll be in the ceiling duct holding the rope that you'll be dangling from."

She'd seen this plot before, and Tom Cruise had played her part. "You stole this whole operation from *Mission Impossible*."

"Actually, they got the idea from *Topkapi*, which, I can tell you from personal experience, really works."

"So you claim," she said.

"You'll find out for yourself in a couple hours."

"Why can't I be the one to hold the rope, and you get to be the dangler?"

"I'm the big strong man. If *you* held the rope you might drop me on my head."

"It would be tempting."

At noon Nick drove a panel van identical to the ones driven by city utility workers into the underground parking structure and went down to the lowest level, the fourth floor. There were almost no cars on this level, and the few that were parked looked as if they'd been there for days. A single surveillance camera was pointed at the elevator and stairwell. Nick parked the van in front of one of the large circular air vents, which was three feet in diameter and partially covered by a metal grate.

Nick and Kate were dressed as city utility workers in white jumpsuits, and wore work gloves, rock-climbing harnesses around their waists, and headbands with tiny headlights attached to them. Kate also wore a backpack containing a rope and pulleys, among other things.

They used the van for cover as they crouched in front of the vent and removed the metal grate. After the grate was removed, they opened the rear doors on the van and pulled out another backpack, and a large handheld masonry saw with vacuum dust control and a circular diamond blade the size of a serving plate. Nick attached the saw to an industrial extension cord and plugged the cord into a nearby outlet. He switched on his headlamp and climbed into the duct, pushing the knapsack with the saw on top of it ahead of them. Kate followed, pulling the grate back into place, crawling along behind Nick.

"How do you know where you're going?" Kate asked Nick.

"I did some research, and I've got a sketch. It's pretty straightforward."

They went a few yards farther and reached a junction with another duct that went up to the vent in the plaza, four stories above their heads.

"X marks the spot," Nick said.

He unzipped the knapsack, removed two respirator masks, goggles, and ear protectors, and handed one set to Kate. He took the saw, lifted it into the duct above his head, and stood. He checked his watch. Two minutes until showtime.

Willie Owens drove along the Cartagena waterfront on Paseo Alfonso XII in a rented Opel Corsa hatchback with the windows rolled down and the music on the radio cranked up as loud it could go.

She headed into the underground garage at the port plaza, stopped at the automated kiosk, and punched the button for a ticket. The gate arm went up. She made sure her seat belt was securely latched and then lifted her foot off the brake and let the car pick up speed as it went down the steep ramp.

The car sped on pure momentum across the first floor of the parking garage and rocketed onto the ramp down to the second level. As she rounded the tight curve without using her brakes, she purposely scraped the car along the wall, shearing off her driver's side mirror and setting off a spray of sparks. The car continued to pick up speed, helped by a tap on the gas pedal.

She shot off the ramp like a batted pinball and grazed a row of parked cars on her driver's side, ripping off fenders and shattering taillights. Car alarms shrieked in her destructive wake.

Willie wrenched the wheel sharply to the right to avoid the next ramp and drove down the next aisle, sideswiping another row of cars along her passenger side. She sheared off her remaining mirror and triggered more alarms before she finally turned the wheel hard to the left and intentionally slammed into the rear of an Audi. She clenched her teeth and squeezed her eyes shut, anticipating the impact. The airbag in her steering wheel burst in her face. She quickly pushed it away and decided that the little car she'd thought might be a hunk of junk was really a lot of fun to drive.

Willie was still extricating herself from the airbag when a security guard wrenched the driver's door open and helped her out of the car. Two more guards arrived, all asking questions, shouting to be heard over the alarms and the music. They were able to turn off the radio, but the car alarms continued to blare, the sound echoing off the concrete walls.

One of the guards helped Willie walk up the ramp to the plaza, where an ambulance was pulling up, siren wailing.

"I'm okay," Willie said, waving the ambulance attendants away. "I don't need a doctor."

"What happened?" the guard asked in halting English, holding her arm to keep her steady.

"The brakes on my rental car went out as I was going down the ramp. I tried to slow myself down by grazing the wall, but it didn't do much good. It's a good thing I signed up for the insurance."

Nick began cutting into the duct the instant he heard the first car alarm. Over the next ten minutes, he cut an opening through the four inches of sheet metal and concrete that was large enough for him and Kate to climb through.

By the time the alarms were extinguished and the chaos in the garage had subsided, Nick and Kate had climbed into an adjoining duct, dropped into a cross duct, and were crawling over the museum ceiling. It was an antiquated system with larger ducts than would be used now, but even at that it was tight.

Nick stopped when he reached the air grate above the conservation room that contained the treasure from the *Nuestra Señora de Santa Maria.* He looked down through the vent, playing his flashlight beam over the rows of hundreds of sealed white plastic buckets full of gold coins.

Kate shrugged out of her backpack, removed a pulley and a battery-operated drill, and handed them to Nick, so he could secure the pulley to the floor of the duct. While he worked with the drill, Kate threaded a coil of rope through the loops in her harness.

"Done," Nick said, discarding the drill.

"Me, too. I'm all looped up."

Kate handed the end of the rope to Nick. He ran it through the pulley, back over his body, and attached it to his harness. He would use his weight to anchor the rope while she lowered herself down to the lab.

Nick removed the air grate, set it aside, and Kate maneuvered herself to the edge of the opening in the duct.

"Have you got a grip on the rope?" she asked.

"I'm ready when you are."

Kate eased through the opening and realized she was loving this. Okay, so it was a little illegal, but she was taking steps to make the world a better place. That was why she'd joined the military. And that was why she'd gone to work for the FBI. It was because she wanted to make a difference.

And as if all this wasn't an odd enough realization, she also admitted that Nick was a good partner. He was smart and strong and reliable. He was everything you would want from a man who was dangling you in midair. True, he could be exasperating and a bit of a loose cannon, but he had good instincts under fire.

She looked back at Nick, gave him a thumbs-up, and slowly

lowered herself to the floor, her headlamp shining a narrow beam of light into the dark room. The buckets were numbered and labeled with grid coordinates indicating where the coins had been found on the debris field. She pulled a collapsible pouch out of her pocket, opened the nearest bucket, and recoiled at the smell.

"Are you okay down there?" Nick asked.

"This water reeks. It's like rotten eggs."

"Good to know. For a minute there I thought it might be you."

Kate gave him a stiff middle finger and was about to stick her gloved hand into a bucket when the lab door crashed open.

12

A man and a woman came into the conservation lab They were kissing and groping, not looking in Kate's direction. The door closed as quickly as it had opened, and the room was plunged into total darkness. Kate's heart skipped a couple beats. She snapped off her headlamp, dropped to the floor, and slithered behind a cluster of buckets. She could hear fumbling and grunting and clothes getting discarded.

The overhead lights flashed on, revealing that the woman was now naked and the man bare-assed, with his pants down around his ankles. Kate couldn't believe this was happening. It was like being in a porn movie.

The lights had come on because the guy had the woman backed up to the light switch. The woman moved and the lights went out. After a moment the lights came on again and Kate saw that the woman had her legs wrapped around the guy's waist. He pushed into her, slamming her against the wall, and the lights went out.

Crap on a cracker, Kate thought. Could it get any worse?

Bang. The lights went on. Every time the guy slammed the woman into the wall, the lights would turn on or off. *Bang, flash. Bang, flash.* The pace picked up, and Kate thought if the flashes didn't stop soon she'd have a seizure.

She heard muffled laughter in the vent above her and decided it was a good thing she didn't have a gun because she would for sure shoot someone . . . possibly Nick.

There was a last big *bang,* the room went dark, and there was a moment of silence. Someone sighed and Kate assumed it was the woman, who had to have a headache after all the wall banging. There was some shuffling around and the rustle of clothes getting pulled on. No words were spoken. The door was eased open, the man peeked out, and something was whispered, but Kate couldn't catch it. The man and woman slipped out of the room and closed the door.

Kate blew out a sigh of relief. She grabbed a chunk of coins out of a bucket and carefully stuffed it into her pouch, thinking the clumps of coins were stuck together in bits of rock like chocolate chips in a cookie. She took a couple more chunks, put the lid back on the bucket, and clipped the bag of coins to her belt with a carabiner. She was on the rope, midway to the vent, when the door suddenly opened again, spilling in light and exposing her hanging from the ceiling.

It was the man. He turned on the light and began searching the floor around the door and under the light switch.

Kate hung as still as she could, utterly exposed, willing the man not to raise his head and look deeper into the room.

He spotted something, reached between two buckets, and picked up a laminated ID badge. He clipped it to the lapel of his lab coat, turned his back to the room to kill the light, and paused.

Damnation, Kate thought. Now what?

The man felt all his pockets and checked to make sure he was zipped up. He turned the light off, and walked out.

Kate wasted no time climbing the rest of the way up the rope and through the duct opening. She looked at Nick and caught him smiling.

"Really?" she said to him.

"You're lucky I didn't completely lose it. When he started slamming her into the light switch I almost fell out of the ceiling."

"It was freaking frightening! And it was *icky.* I'm going to have to pour bleach into my brain."

Nick reached out and hauled her across the opening in the duct so that she was on his side of the air vent. He kissed her on the top of her head and flipped her light on. "You've led a sheltered life."

"Not true," Kate said. "I saw two dogs doing the deed in a parking lot once, and they were stuck together when they were done."

"Forever?"

"For about ten minutes. They weren't happy about it."

"You do the crime, you pay the time," Nick said. He replaced the vent and glued it in place. "Let's move out."

They made their way back through the duct toward the garage, gathering up their equipment as they went along and patching the hole they'd cut.

They packed everything into the van, replaced the vent, and drove up to the second level of the garage, where police officers were busy taking reports from angry car owners. A tow truck was hitching up Willie's bashed-up Opel. A police officer stepped in front of their van and cleared a path for them through the crowd. Kate tried to look tired, bored, and unmemorable in the passenger seat and apparently succeeded. The cop didn't seem to notice her.

Nick nodded and smiled his thanks to the officer, drove up the ramp to the first floor, and then out of the garage, into the sunshine on Paseo Alfonso XII.

An hour later, Nick parked the van on a dirt road in the forested countryside. They wiped the van down for prints and left their jumpsuits and the ignition key inside. Kate carried the bag of gold to a Renault hatchback Nick had hidden previously in the trees. She put the bag of gold in one of the suitcases in the trunk.

Nick got behind the wheel and took them to the A-92 freeway for the 582-mile drive to Lisbon. They stopped four and a half hours later at a gas station to refill the Renault's tank, stretch their legs, get some food, and change drivers.

"We're going to be passing close to Seville," Nick said to Kate. "We should take a detour and make a stop at my favorite tapas bar. It's a little place in the old town, and it serves the most extraordinary *Jabugo pata negra bellota*."

Kate was driving with one hand on the wheel and the other hand stuffed into a bag of Vicente Vidal *patatas fritas sabor jamón*. She'd gotten the *patatas fritas* when they'd stopped at the gas station, and they were the most awesome potato chips she'd ever eaten.

"I've never heard of Jabugo whatever," Kate said. "It sounds awful."

"It's cured ham from pigs raised in the mountain village of Jabugo and fed only acorns."

"By hand, I suppose. By virgins."

"You have no appreciation for fine cuisine," he said.

"I'm eating prosciutto-flavored potato chips fried in olive oil."

"That's not fine cuisine."

"It is where I come from. Having dinner tonight in a fancy restaurant would mean leaving the car parked on the street with hundreds of thousands of dollars of gold coins in the trunk. I'd rather not take the chance just so you can have a gourmet dinner."

"Tapas isn't gourmet," he said. "Think of it as high-quality fast food."

"Can you get it at a drive-through?"

"No."

"Then it isn't fast food," she said. "It's slow food."

"So are you going to take the turnoff to Seville?"

"Absolutely. I'm all about acorn ham."

They crossed the border into Portugal and arrived in Lisbon shortly after midnight, approaching the city from the south on the Ponte 25 de Abril. It was a half-mile-long replica of the Golden Gate Bridge spanning the Rio Tejo, the gateway to the Atlantic. A Golden Gate Bridge clone was a good fit for Lisbon, which, like San Francisco, is a coastal city built on steep hills and once devastated by a massive earthquake. The Lisbon temblor hit on November 1, 1755, and was immediately followed by a huge tidal wave and then a hellacious inferno sparked by cooking fires. The fires lasted for five days and destroyed two-thirds of the city, which still bore the scars more than two centuries later.

Once off the bridge, Kate headed east along the riverfront, past the historic city center to the decaying industrial area.

Running along Rua Cintura do Porto behind a high graffiti-covered stone wall topped with razor wire was a derelict, trash-strewn gravel yard with a rotting wharf jutting out into the river. The gate to the property was open. A rutted dirt road lined with tall, dry weeds led to the wharf, where a 150-foot cargo ship was docked.

The ship had a low main deck, close to the water, and a high proud bow. The crane attached to the deck resembled a claw raised in fury, raging against the moon. The three-story deck-house was aft. The bridge atop the deckhouse was dark, but a few windows were lit on the floors below, where the cabins, galley, and mess were located.

Kate drove down the road that cut through the lot, the car bouncing and rocking over the uneven ground. As she got closer to the ship, she could see sparks from someone welding on the deck near the crane. She parked beside a pickup truck and a van and got out with Nick, who lifted the hatchback and took out the suitcase full of gold.

They walked to the end of the wharf, and floodlights flashed on atop the crane and the deckhouse, illuminating the boat deck and the steep gangway. Kate and Nick trudged up the gangway and were met on deck by Jake.

"Welcome aboard the *Seaquest,*" Jake said. "How'd it go in Cartagena?"

"We've got the gold," Nick said. "Your daughter has the makings of a master thief."

"That's my girl," Jake said.

"That's not me at all," she said, kissing her dad on the cheek. "I'd much prefer to arrest thieves than be one. There's a lasting sense of accomplishment that only comes from a deep, methodical investigation."

"You sound like the keynote speaker at a proctology conference," Jake said. "And by the way, I'm clean as a whistle."

Nick grinned. "Congratulations."

"Yeah, Dad, that's great."

"I suppose," Jake said, "but I feel like I didn't get my money's worth. I was sort of hoping they'd at least find a polyp."

They all crossed the deck to where Tom was working. He was welding a tail fin onto what looked like an enormous mechanical shark with floodlights for eyes, a surveillance camera on his nose, and a basket for collecting treasure where his mouth was supposed to be.

Tom turned off the torch, lifted up his protective mask, and took a step back to admire his creation. "I know it looks rough, but I haven't added the robotic claw or put all the bling on it yet."

"What bling?" Kate asked.

"The chrome and blinky lights," Nick said.

"That's a remotely operated submersible survey vehicle," Kate said. "Why does it need chrome and blinking lights?"

"The same reason you used cleavage as bait for the bank robbers," Nick said. "You knew it would get their attention. If Menendez is hooked by the sub, he'll go along with everything else."

"Wait until you see it with the nacelles," Tom said.

"What are nacelles?" Kate asked.

"The two big, badass tubes on the back of the starship *Enterprise* that hold the propulsion system," Tom said. "Only these will be a lot smaller, like the ones on the bottom of the

Enterprise's shuttle craft. Are you ready to see how the command center is coming along?"

"Absolutely," Nick said. "Lead the way."

They took the metal stairs to the second level and entered a narrow corridor leading to a conference room dominated by a large boomerang-shaped control panel. The control panel was crammed with a keyboard and an array of knobs, dials, and multicolored buttons. At the center of it all, in front of a console with a forty-inch monitor flanked by several smaller ones, was a joystick that could have come from a fighter jet. There were two smaller joysticks on either side of it.

"Let me guess," Kate said, gesturing to the center joystick, "our sub fires missiles, too."

The three men stared at her like she was an idiot, but it was Nick who spoke up. "Why would a remotely operated vehicle have missiles?"

"Why would it have nacelles?"

"To make it go."

"It has propellers for that," Kate said.

"In the nacelles," Nick said.

"What are they doing in there?"

"Looking a lot cooler than propellers that aren't in nacelles."

"So if the ROV doesn't fire weapons," Kate said, "why do you have a such an elaborate joystick?"

"So it looks fun to drive," Nick said.

Tom hit a switch somewhere and the multicolored buttons

on the control panel lit up and the console began blinking like a Christmas tree.

Jake nodded. "Very impressive."

"It's silly," Kate said. "What are all the lighted buttons supposed to do?"

"Blink," Tom said.

"What I mean is, in the real world, what are they supposed to control?"

"Nothing," Nick said.

"Then why do we have them?"

"Have you ever watched *Star Trek* or *Battlestar Galactica*?" Nick asked.

"Sure."

"Well the bridges on those starships are loaded with blinking lights that have absolutely no function and lots of monitors with meaningless readouts constantly scrolling on the screen."

"This isn't a starship," Kate said.

"But it has to look like one or Menendez won't be impressed. Authenticity is not what we are going for here," Nick said. "It's creating a fantasy that Menendez can't resist. We don't want him thinking. We want him dreaming."

"Nick is right," Tom said. "If there's one thing I've learned building treehouses, it's that all men are kids at heart. They will jump at any opportunity to fulfill their childhood fantasies. Hell, that's why I'm here."

"What fantasy is this for you?" Kate asked.

"Tom Underhill, fearless samurai, living a life of intrigue in exotic locales."

"You're on an old cargo ship docked at an abandoned gravel yard," Kate said.

"I'm on a boat in Lisbon with three deadly mercenaries, a master of disguise, a secret agent, and a mysterious security guy."

"I'm not a secret agent," Kate said.

"I'm married with two kids," Tom said. "I live in Rancho Cucamonga, and I build treehouses for a living. Don't rain on my parade."

13

Jake took Nick and Kate to the ship's mess so they could meet Billy Dee Snipes.

Billy Dee was sitting at a table, smoking a cigar. He looked like a skeleton that had been painted black, dressed in a blue tracksuit, and propped in a chair facing the door to startle people. Kate's first thought was that the man was either dying of some horrible disease or was at the end of a long hunger strike.

"Billy Dee Snipes," Jake said. "This is my daughter Kate and her associate Nick."

Billy Dee stood up and shook hands with them both. For a man with a skeletal hand, Billy Dee had a surprisingly strong grip.

"Thanks for helping us out on this," Kate said. "We really appreciate it."

"My pleasure, but if you'd come to me earlier, I could have *hijacked* a boat like this for you and saved you a lot of money."

"You did hijack this boat," Jake said. "Only it was twenty years ago."

"I'll be damned," Billy Dee said. "You found my mark?"

Jake nodded. "There's a tiny skull and crossbones carved into the bulkhead up on the bridge."

"Then this was meant to be." Billy Dee reached for Nick's suitcase. "I'm thinking you must have the treasure in the suitcase, so I'll take it off your hands for safekeeping."

"Where's it going?" Kate asked.

"It's staying here on the boat, in a bucket of water under my cot. I sleep with my machete under my pillow, and I assure you that I am a very light sleeper."

"I would be, too, if there was a chance I'd roll over on a machete," Nick said.

"It's safer than sharing the bed with a woman," Billy Dee said, then smiled at Kate. "No offense, my dear."

"None taken," Kate said.

Nick grinned. "Kate prefers a loaded gun next to her bed."

"Is that all?" Jake asked Kate. "Where's your hand grenade?"

"I don't have a hand grenade."

"What happened to the one I gave you for Christmas?"

"I forgot about that," she said. "I guess it's around the apartment somewhere."

"You lost a hand grenade in your apartment?" Nick said. "Next time I visit I'll be more careful."

"*Next time?*" Kate narrowed her eyes at him. "I've never invited you over. You jerk! You broke into my apartment, didn't you?"

"That's what you get for not having it properly booby-trapped," Jake said.

Nick handed the suitcase over to Billy Dee and turned to Jake. "Shall we meet the other new member of our crew?"

Everyone trooped to the engine room, and as they got closer, they could hear the clanging of tools against metal and Barnacle Bob singing an ancient sea shanty in a heavy, almost incomprehensible cockney accent. *"What will we do with a drunken sailor, what will we do with a drunken sailor, what will we do with a drunken sailor, early in the morning?"*

It was hot and humid in the dimly lit room, and there were hundreds of engine parts all over the floor. Standing amid it all, covered in oil and grease like a pig who'd been rolling in mud, was Barnacle Bob, singing away.

"Way hay and up she rises, way hay and up she rises, way hay and up she rises, early in the morning . . ."

Barnacle Bob, with his squarish, flat-topped head, jutting jaw, and no neck, resembled a cartoon character after a boulder has been dropped on him. He had broad shoulders, and a big belly over a narrow waist and thin legs, as if his belt had been cinched way, way too tight. He banged a tool against a pipe in time with his singing.

"Bob, I'd like you to meet my daughter Kate and her associate Nick," Jake yelled over the singing and clanging. "They're running this operation."

Bob looked dubious.

"It looks like you've dismantled the engine," Kate said.

"That's what I did, guv."

"But I thought that it was recently rebuilt."

"Not by me. An engine is like a woman. I have to get to know her. Only way to do that is to get under her skirt."

"Have you tried talking?" Kate said.

"To an engine?" Bob asked.

"To a woman."

"Why would I want to do that?"

"I'm a woman. You're talking to me."

"You're Jake's daughter. I'm not going to shag you."

"That's for sure," Kate said.

"Glad we got that out of the way," Jake said. "Is she in good shape?"

"If you want it slow and steady, she'll do fine. If you want it fast and hard, she'll pass out in the middle and leave you hanging."

"Just to clarify," Kate said, "we're talking about his opinion of the boat now, right?"

"Will she be ready to go this week?" Nick asked.

"Dressed up pretty with lipstick on."

"That's what I like to hear," Nick said. "Carry on."

Bob went back to work and to singing. *"Give him a dose of salt and water, give him a dose of salt and water . . ."*

Nick, Kate, and Jake headed back on deck.

"Where's Boyd?" Nick asked.

Jake gestured to the bridge. "He's been holed up in there since he arrived a few days ago."

"There are no lights on," Kate said.

"It's part of his method," Jake said.

"He's a nut," Kate said.

Nick slid his arm around her shoulders and hugged her into him. "True enough, Pumpkin, but he's *our* nut."

The moon cast enough light through the bridge's wraparound windows that Nick and Kate could see Boyd standing at the captain's station at the control panel. His back was to them as he looked out over the bow.

"Hey, Boyd," Kate said. "What are you doing up here?"

"Becoming at home with the set. As captain of the *Seaquest,* I need to be completely and naturally at ease on my bridge. I need to be able to express that comfort, and command of my environment, unconsciously in my body language."

"Why don't you turn on the lights?"

"So I can learn to find my way blind. Knowing my way around the bridge has to become instinctive. That's how intimately the captain knows this ship."

"Well, I don't know the ship at all, and I don't want to crash into something."

Kate searched the wall until she found a light switch and flicked it on. The bridge was clean and modern, the control panel packed with all the latest equipment. But Kate was familiar enough with a ship's bridge that she could see that Tom had augmented the standard engine, sonar, communications, and navigation controls, screens, and gauges with lots of extra buttons and lights.

Boyd still had his back to them. He wore a white captain's cap, a white short-sleeved shirt with striped epaulets, pressed white slacks, and black deck shoes buffed to a glossy sheen.

"Nice uniform," Nick said. "But why are you wearing it now? We're a week away from showtime."

"Captain Bridger always wears his uniform, and I need to be comfortable in the man's skin."

"I see," Nick said. "I admire your preparation for a job."

"Acting is not a job, Nick. It's an art." Boyd turned around, and now they could see he wore a black eye patch over his left eye and a full, but well trimmed, gray-flecked beard that had to be a fake, since he hadn't had time to grow it.

"What's with the eye patch?" Kate asked.

"The captain lost his eye in the horrible tragedy that drove him to the sea, where he wanders endlessly in self-imposed exile, alone in his personal sorrow." Boyd got choked up. He cleared his throat. "Sorry, I get emotional every time I think about it."

Nick nodded and spoke softly. "Take your time."

"Oh, for God's sake," Kate said. "The captain is not real. He's a figment of your imagination."

"Not anymore." Boyd waved a hand over his body. "He lives through me."

"Vividly," Nick said. "It's a complete and utterly convincing transformation."

Not to Kate. She crossed her arms under her chest, standing her ground. "You don't think the eye patch is a cliché?"

Nick shook his head. "A great actor can turn cliché into revelation. And Boyd has done that."

Kate almost coughed up her prosciutto potato chips. "Why the beard?"

"It's the mask the captain wears to hide his pain from others," Boyd said, limping toward them.

Kate groaned. "Please don't tell me he's got a peg leg, too."

"Of course not. I keep banging my knee. It's not easy moving around in the dark with only one good eye. But I know that pain is part of the process."

The sweep of headlights from a car turning off the boulevard into the empty lot below caught their attention. Kate found binoculars on the navigation desk and looked out the window. A bright red Ferrari was streaking toward the wharf at high speed.

Nick closed his eyes as he listened to the car's throaty roar. "I know that sound. It's a 4.5-liter naturally aspirated V8 with a distinct Italian accent, definitely a Ferrari 458." He opened his eyes and smiled at Kate. "A red one."

Boyd glanced out the window, and then looked back at

Nick incredulously. "You can tell all that from the sound of the engine?"

"Could you tell the difference between Frank Sinatra and Justin Bieber singing 'My Way'?"

"Of course," Boyd said.

"Well, there you go."

The three of them went down to the deck to greet the new arrival, with Boyd stumbling a few times, the eye patch throwing off his vision.

"I got here as fast as I could," Willie said. "I hit a hundred and forty miles per hour on a couple stretches." Willie tossed Nick the keys. He caught them with one hand. "I broke the car in for you, so don't be gentle."

Kate turned to him. "Where are you going?"

"To my hotel, of course. It's getting late and I'm bushed."

"I thought we were all bunking on the boat."

"I've booked a suite at the Vincenzo Palace."

"Does it have to be a palace? Why not a Sheraton?"

"I've got to establish my cover. I'm Nick Hartley, a very successful treasure hunter looking for a deep-pocketed and unscrupulous investor to fund the salvage of my latest find, a shipwreck laden with five hundred million dollars in gold. If I'm as good as I say I am, then I've got money, and I'd be flaunting it by staying at one of the very best hotels in Lisbon. I don't search for treasure to live frugally."

"You're an actor at heart. No wonder you understand me so

well," Boyd said. "And like a true professional, you fully embody the roles that you play."

"He does if the role involves wearing the best clothes, driving the fanciest cars, and staying in the most luxurious hotels," Kate said. "You won't see him pretending to be a homeless guy."

"Unfortunately, I've been typecast by my good looks and my innate sense of style," Nick said. "It's a burden I try to live with." He crooked a finger at Kate. "Could I speak to you privately a moment?"

Kate followed him out to the deck. "Is there a problem?"

He tucked a wisp of hair that had come loose from Kate's ponytail behind her ear. "No problem. I just thought you might need a private moment to get used to being married."

"Say what?"

"From this moment on, we're Nick and Kate Hartley, greedy archaeologists. And of course we cohabit, since we're married."

"I don't think so."

"Your choice, but if we aren't husband and wife, I'll have to go alone into the lion's den. And you'll miss all the fun."

"Why do we have to be husband and wife?"

"It's a believable cover."

Kate narrowed her eyes. "How far does this husband-and-wife thing go?"

"As far as you want it to go."

Oh crap, Kate thought. That wasn't good. She had occasional thoughts about him. Thoughts that didn't sit well with her job or her dedication to law and order. Thoughts that got her all warm and mushy inside.

"Will I have my own bedroom?" she asked him.

"If that's what you prefer. It's a two-bedroom suite."

"I suppose it will be okay then."

Nick took a simple platinum band out of his pocket and slipped it on Kate's ring finger. "Now it's official."

Kate stared at the band with equal parts horror and terrifying happiness. The happiness was sitting like a tennis ball in her throat and sending flashes of fire across her chest. No one had put a ring on her finger before. Actually, someone had tried several years ago, but she'd broken his hand. Not intentionally. It had been one of those reflex reactions.

This is pretend, she told herself. Get a grip. This is the job, for crying out loud. And if you ever do get married for real, it's not going to be to a man on the FBI's Ten Most Wanted list!

"This sort of caught me by surprise," she said to Nick.

"I've never been a fan of long engagements."

"I get that," Kate said, "but you realize you're going to have to explain this to my dad."

14

Kate sat on her comfy bed in her comfy bedroom in her luxurious suite and called Carl Jessup on her cellphone. She wanted to get him at the office before he went home. It was almost 6 P.M. the previous day in Los Angeles. Kate filled him in on her progress in the broadest possible terms and without mentioning any names.

"My work in Spain is complete," she said. "My investigation has taken me to Lisbon."

She wasn't about to admit to any heists, or aiding a wanted fugitive, or any other illegal activity on a phone line routed through the federal building. The National Security Agency had offices in the building, too.

"It sounds like you are on the hunt," Jessup said. "What can we do to help?"

"I need someone to do some research for me."

"I'll put Ryerson on it," Jessup said.

"He's not going to like running investigative errands for me."

"It's not for you, it's for the Bureau. Besides, you want our best man on this."

"I'm your best man," Kate said.

"Second best, then. Hold on a sec. I'll bring him in here and put you on the speaker." She waited for a moment, and then heard Ryerson come in. Jessup spoke again. "Okay, Kate, I've got Seth here with me. Bring us up to speed."

"Greetings from Lisbon."

"Really? She's in *Lisbon*?" Ryerson said. "The most exotic place I've been sent on assignment is Duluth."

"Kate is over there on Nick Fox's trail," Jessup said.

"I thought the thief turned out to be a Nick Fox copycat."

"She was," Kate said. "Her name is Serena Blake and she used to work with Fox. That's why she thought she could commit a string of crimes and pin them on him."

"So case closed," Ryerson said.

"Not quite," Kate said. "Serena is facing prison stretches now in four countries, so she was desperate to cut a deal with us. I told her unless she had something on Fox, I wasn't interested. Turns out she had a tidbit. She says he's in business with Lester Menendez on some kind of plot. If we can find Menendez, we'll find Fox."

"Menendez is a ghost," Ryerson said. "He's even more elusive than Fox. With all due respect, there's no place to start."

"There's the chocolate," Kate said.

"Oh, no, not that again," Ryerson said. "Just because I disagree with you on this, that's no excuse to throw accusations at me. How many times do I have to tell you? I didn't take your precious half-pound bag of M&M's. I wouldn't go near your cubicle unless a HazMat team cleared it first."

"I know you took them. I'm a crack FBI investigator, but that's not the chocolate I'm talking about. Menendez loves fine chocolate. He goes for the rarest, purest, and most expensive chocolate there is. I don't think he's lost his taste for it just because he has a new face and body. I need you to find the people who make that chocolate and get me a list of their European customers."

"There will be hundreds of names, maybe thousands. How will you know which one of them is Menendez?" Ryerson asked.

"I won't, but I'm working on it. That's why I am in Lisbon. My sources tell me Fox is here. If he is, Menendez may be nearby, too. If I can find out who Fox contacts, I can compare the names to the list."

"I think she might be on to something," Jessup said to Ryerson. "I think it's worth a few hours of your time. Get her those names as soon as possible."

"Yes, sir," Ryerson said, not sounding all that happy.

Modern downtown Lisbon, the Baixa, lies in a valley that runs south to the Tejo riverfront, where it ends at the Praça do Comércio, once a scenic spot for public executions. The royal palace also stood there before the earthquake, tsunami, and fire of 1755 wiped it away in what many at the time believed was a heavy-handed message from God.

The hill on the east edge of the city is topped by the restored ruins of the Castelo de São Jorge. Sloping away from the castle, the Alfama district is a tightly packed medieval maze of crooked buildings. The buildings lean against one another like staggering drunks trying to keep their balance on the steep cobbled streets. Laundry lines hang across the streets, and the air is thick with the smell of cooking fat.

On the hill to the west is the Bairro Alto, the "upper district," which is no less densely packed, but is substantially wealthier. Its narrow streets are laid out in an orderly grid with expensive houses, restaurants, art galleries, and shops for the rich. The Bairro Alto is the bohemian and artistic heart of Lisbon, where crowds pack the tiny streets and steps at night drinking, carousing, and relieving themselves outside the countless tiny taverns and *fado* houses. Performers, waiters, and the hungry homeless sing loudly and mournfully in the *fado* houses, expressing their bluesy unending longing for what was and what can never be. The songs merge together into a sorrowful, chilly breeze of cigarette smoke and salty fish aroma that drift up to the top of Bairro Alto.

Kate took it all in while she waited for Nick outside the ornate yellow Vincenzo Palace hotel, once the opulent home of Count Vincenzo, the sardine king of Lisbon.

"Hard to believe, but you almost look happy to see me," Nick said, greeting Kate with a friendly kiss on the cheek.

"I read about *fado* in my guidebook, but now that I'm hearing it I don't get it."

"It's like mariachi, only the singers who come to your table are wearing black and they're joyless."

Nick led her around the corner and down the slender Rua das Flores, which ran alongside the steep Rua do Alecrim, the Bairro Alto's major north-south boulevard, all the way to the waterfront.

"The man we're seeing to help get the word out in the underworld about our treasure is a *fado* singer," Nick said.

"His name?"

"Diogo Alves."

"You say that like his name is supposed to mean something to me."

Nick sighed. "Don't they teach you anything at Quantico? Northwest of here, there is the Aqueduto das Águas Livres, a 213-foot-tall eighteenth-century aqueduct that spans the Alcântara valley. It used to bring fresh water to the city and served as a bridge for traveling vegetable merchants. In the late 1830s, over the course of several years, over seventy people plunged to their deaths from the aqueduct in a wave of baffling suicides."

"There must have been a *fado* singer on the aqueduct. What does that ancient history have to do with Diogo Alves?"

"It wasn't until four members of the same family killed themselves that authorities began to suspect something was amiss. Turns out those seventy people were robbed and thrown off the aqueduct by Diogo Alves, Portugal's first recorded serial killer and still the worst. Alves was hanged in 1841 and was considered so supremely evil that his head was chopped off and put in a jar of formaldehyde for scientific study. The aqueduct has been closed to foot traffic ever since."

As they walked closer to the waterfront, the crowds thinned, and the brightly painted buildings with elaborate ironwork and colorful flowerpots gave way to peeling paint, boarded-up windows, rusted wrought-iron bars, and graffiti-covered walls. The shadows thickened, the night became darker, and they were alone. Nick seemed cheerfully oblivious to the danger in the air. Kate wasn't. All her senses were heightened. The story Nick told as they descended into the darkness hadn't helped.

"I hope the Diogo Alves that we're meeting tonight isn't a headless reanimated corpse," Kate said.

"Diogo is a distant relative of the serial killer. He owns a sleazy bar at the waterfront, sings *fado* to the customers, and works as a talent agent for crooks. He makes introductions and organizes crimes for a small cut of the action. He's also known as the law among the lawless, resolving disagreements and passing judgment on offenders."

"They're all offenders."

"There are always rules," Nick said. "If there's a killing among crooks, Diogo is the one who decides if it was justified. If he decides it wasn't, he carries out the punishment himself."

"What kind of punishment?"

"He likes to toss people from very high places."

"Lovely," Kate said.

"We'll be fine. We haven't killed anyone. We're just here to do business. If we want to get word to Menendez, Diogo is the person in Lisbon who can do it."

A few blocks from the waterfront they hit Rua Nova do Carvalho. A half block to the east, Rua do Alecrim began its ascent to Bairro Alto by bridging over a warren of seedy and dangerous-looking streets. The area once teemed with sailors looking to satisfy their desires in dive bars with names that evoked their faraway homes. The Oslo. The Copenhagen. The Texas. The Jamaican.

The crowds of sailors had faded away decades ago, and the few bars that remained catered to drunks, drug addicts, prostitutes, and sexual tourists. Tonight the street was deserted, the breeze kicking up bits of trash as if they were fallen leaves.

Nick gestured to the tunnel where Rua Nova do Carvalho passed under the Rua do Alecrim. "Diogo's bar, the Slam, is through there, on the other side."

"Of course it is," Kate said, putting her hand in her jacket pocket, taking hold of a miniature telescoping baton.

Nick strolled into the tunnel, and Kate followed cautiously a few steps behind him. Before entering the tunnel she noted the dark alley to her left, and the steps up the hill to her right. Light inside the tunnel was dim to nonexistent. The sick yellow glow of a streetlight could be seen at the far end.

Kate's eyes adjusted to the darkness just as two figures peeled away from the walls, like shadows come to life, to block their path. She sensed one more man coming out of hiding behind her and Nick.

One of the men in front of them wore a white tank top and droopy jeans. All of his visible skin was tattooed. She couldn't see all of his tattoos in the lousy light, but it was hard to miss the dead goat etched across his bald head, the devil's horns on his forehead, the tears at the corners of his eyes, the tombstone on his throat, and the daggers on his cheeks. She couldn't see what the other guy looked like, only his silhouette.

Tattoo spat out some words in Portuguese that were laced with menace and the promise of violence. Nick responded affably in Portuguese as well, a smile on his face. Kate stepped up beside him, keeping her eyes on Tattoo.

"What does he want?" Kate asked.

"He wants us to pay a toll to pass, but I find the charge unreasonable. I offered to buy him and his friends a drink at the Slam instead. Or at least I think I did. My Portuguese isn't great."

"What's the toll?"

Tattoo grinned, showing off a gold tooth, and took a straight razor out of his back pocket. "His money and your body," he said in English.

"I'll make you a deal," Kate said. "You and your friends step aside now and I won't break your jaw."

Before Tattoo could reply, she yanked her hand out of her pocket and whipped open the baton, which instantly telescoped out from palm-size to twelve inches of tempered bone-cracking steel. The baton was small, but the dramatic value of simply brandishing it and extending it was considerable.

Tattoo instinctively reared back in surprise, but when he saw how short the baton was, he grinned and stepped toward her.

"I'm going to take that little stick from you and—"

Kate acted before he could finish his threat. She swatted him across the face, breaking his jaw and slashing his cheek open. The pain and shock made him drop the razor, which she kicked aside as she spun around to take out the man behind her, who was charging at her with a switchblade.

The thug who'd been standing next to Tattoo took a swing at Nick. Nick calmly ducked under the blow and drove his fist deep into the man's gut. The thug dropped to his knees, all the wind escaping from him like a deflating balloon.

Kate sidestepped the other assailant's blade, and whacked him in the kidney with her baton as he passed, and then once again across his back for good measure, knocking him face-first to the ground.

She returned to a fighting stance, checking to see if any of the three men were ready for more. Two of them were on the ground and Tattoo was staggering around, clutching his bleeding face and moaning. The fight was over, about sixty seconds after it began. She turned to the wall, pressed her baton closed against it, and put the weapon back into her pocket.

"Handy little toy you have there," Nick said. "Good thing I'm secure in my manliness, or I might find you intimidating."

15

The Slam was only a few yards from the tunnel opening. The lightbulbs on the sign had burned out decades ago, and blue paint was peeling off the centuries-old building like flecks of dried skin.

Nick opened the door to the Slam, and they stepped inside. The bar was small, holding only a few dozen tables. The low ceiling trapped the smoke from the cigarettes, cigars, and joints so that it hung in the air like a dense fog. The walls and sagging shelves were crammed with countless knickknacks, gathered over decades, perhaps even centuries, from the bar's patrons. Wood carvings. Nautical maps. Vases. Model boats. Daggers. Snow globes. Stuffed animals. Porcelain. Old radios. Carved ivory. An Ultraman doll. African fertility idols. It was like an

JANET EVANOVICH AND LEE GOLDBERG

eclectic antiques store that also served watered-down alcohol and rancid salted cod.

The clientele were scarred, tattooed, hard-looking men and women whose faces and hollow gazes reflected lives of crime, cruelty, poverty, and bitterness. But now those eyes were all filled with tears and locked on the *fadista,* Diogo Alves, a short man dressed in black with a pear-shaped face and a pencil mustache, who stood in front of the long tiled bar. A slender, ghostly pale woman draped in a black shawl sat on a barstool behind him and strummed a Portuguese *guitarra* while staring at the floor with the emptiness of someone who no longer had a reason, or the will, to live.

"Diogo is not exactly Michael Bublé," Kate said.

"*Fado* is less about a good voice than it is about the emotion behind the words."

"What's he singing about?"

"How love is a flesh-eating disease that slowly devours your heart but you can't stop hungering for more, even as it's killing you."

"I don't think anybody will be whistling that tune at work tomorrow."

Alves finished his song and lowered his head. He was five foot two without his lifts. All the emotion he'd dredged up for his *fado* had brought beads of sweat to his brow, which he dabbed away with a black silk handkerchief. The *guitarrista* looked like she was ready to take a guitar string and garrote herself with it.

The customers applauded and, as the applause died down,

people began talking, drinking, and laughing again, like a paused recording that had been restarted to play at high volume.

"Try not to look so tough," Nick whispered. "Remember, we're greedy underwater archaeologists."

"Indiana Jones is an archaeologist and he's tough."

"He's an exception," Nick said and moved toward Alves with Kate following close on his heels.

The bartender served Alves an *uma bica,* a small cup of strong black coffee, and Alves drank it in a single shot.

"May I have a word, Mr. Alves?" Nick asked.

Alves glanced over at Nick. "Do I know you?"

Nick tossed a gold coin onto the bar. It was one of the Spanish doubloons they'd stolen in Cartagena, and it was still caked with concretions. "I've found three hundred tons of those, and much, much more, at the bottom of the sea off the coast of Portugal, but I don't have the resources to bring them up."

Alves picked up the coin and examined it. "You could go to the Spanish government."

"They could take it away from me and not pay me anything," Nick said. "Then we'd all lose."

"What would I lose?"

"A cool million for putting me together with the right person."

Alves sniffed the coin, as if the dead fish smell would somehow reveal its worth or the potential of the deal. "I didn't get your name."

"I'm Nick Hartley," Nick said and took Kate's hand. "This is my wife, Kate."

Alves smiled. "A beautiful name for a beautiful woman. And I do love beautiful women. It's a failing of mine. A sickness, really. I love women too much. You'd know if you understood my song. I've been married and divorced six times."

"That's a lot of alimony," Kate said.

"Not really," he said. "They're all dead."

"That's a serious divorce," Kate said.

"I believe in a clean break." Alves laughed and nodded with delight. "I like your wife, Nick. She's tough. You should hold on to her."

"I'm trying," Nick said.

Alves snapped his fingers to get the bartender's attention and then gestured to Nick and Kate to join him in a dark booth in a corner. Nick and Kate sat on one side of the table, Alves on the other, and the bartender brought over a bottle of wine and three glasses.

"What is your line of work?" Alves asked while the bartender poured wine in his glass.

"Archaeologists by training," Nick said. "Treasure hunters by trade."

Alves sipped the wine, nodded in approval, and waved the bartender away.

"How did you find me?" Alves asked, pouring the wine for Kate and Nick.

"I make it my business to know the people who can get

things done wherever I go," Nick said. "Duff MacTaggert gave me your name."

Duff was Nick's former mentor, a legendary thief who'd retired to pampered seclusion on an Indonesian island that had once belonged to imprisoned financier Derek Griffin. The tropical island retreat was something Nick had arranged for Duff to repay a favor. It wouldn't be easy for Alves to reach Duff to confirm the recommendation, though Kate was sure Nick had prepared Duff for the call anyway. She was also certain that Nick's dependable tech guru in Hong Kong had prepared a thorough Web history for the Hartleys if Alves wanted to Google them.

Alves spun the gold coin on the table. "Tell me more about the treasure you've found."

"It's the *Santa Isabel*," Nick said.

At the mention of the name Alves caught his breath.

"You're familiar with it?" Nick asked.

"Of course. Lisbon is a city built on riches we obtained from exploring the seas. We established the spice trade, so you can thank the Portuguese for your Cinnabons, and we mined untold riches in gold and silver in the New World. So we know all about the lost treasure galleons, and the *Santa Isabel* is, perhaps, the most legendary one of all. She was only days away from Spain when she sank in a fierce storm with her gigantic cargo of gold, perhaps the largest bounty ever contained on a single vessel. For centuries, people have searched for that ship. What makes you think that you've found it?"

Nick took a sip of wine. "Because it's the only ship I know that went down with a one-ton table made of solid gold and a thousand-piece gold dinner set. I've seen that table and some of the dishes on the ocean floor."

"If what you say is true, then you've found an incredible fortune beyond any man's wildest dreams," Alves said. "Why share the treasure with anyone else?"

"We've searched for the *Santa Isabel* most of our lives. It's been an obsession. It's cost us almost every penny we have. We don't have the money to recover the treasure. And even if we did, we can't take the chance that the Spanish government will swoop in and take the gold away from us, leaving us with nothing. We want to cash out."

Alves glanced down at the coin that was still lying on the table. "What do you mean by 'cash out'?"

"We figure the treasure is worth about seven hundred million dollars today. We're well aware of the cost and risk involved in salvaging it. So we're willing to sell the location for a mere two and a half percent of the treasure's value."

"Seventeen and a half million dollars is a very large amount of money," Alves said.

"Not large enough," Kate said. "I told Nick that a ten percent commission is the rock-bottom finder's fee in most situations."

"Nobody is going to give us seventy million in cash for a treasure map," Nick said. "We have to be reasonable, honey."

"No, we don't. We've found an unreasonably huge fortune. If nobody wants to pay us what we deserve, we'll pull up just enough coins to live ridiculously well, but not so well we draw attention to ourselves, and leave the rest at the bottom of the sea."

"To cash out, you'll need to find someone with vast amounts of ready cash, but also a high tolerance for risk," Alves said. "That person would also have to be enormously powerful, greatly respected, and deeply feared to have any chance of success. There are only a few men like that in Europe, and they are very dangerous."

"More dangerous than you, Diogo?" Kate asked.

"They are more likely to torture the location from you than pay you for it. I'm tempted myself," Alves said. "So even asking for two and a half percent is probably too bold."

"I have a contingency plan that takes torture off the table," Nick said, "but that's not important right now."

"It is if I want to torture you."

"Do you? Or would you rather earn a million dollars from me and whatever you can get from the buyer and walk away clean, leaving the mess, the risk, and the worry to someone else?"

Alves took a sip of his wine while he considered his options.

"My commission will be one and three-quarters million," he finally said. "As your lovely wife pointed out, ten percent is standard. Taking a mere six percent would be insulting."

Nick gave Alves a slight nod of consent. "I wouldn't want to insult you."

"No, Nick, you wouldn't."

...

Alves agreed to leave word at the Vincenzo Palace when he was ready to meet to discuss possible buyers. Nick told Alves he'd also put the word out in London, Berlin, Paris, and Tangier, so Alves had better not drag his feet. There would be other suitors. That was fine with Alves, who kept the coin and warned Nick and Kate that if there was anything "dishonest" about the deal, the two of them would find themselves at the bottom of the sea, chained to blocks of concrete. After that, Alves excused himself to sing another song, and Nick and Kate left the bar.

"Were you telling the truth about putting out the word in those other cities?" Kate asked when they were on the street.

"Yes, of course. We can't rely only on him to reach Menendez. Even so, I think Alves is our best shot. He does a lot of business in Spain and that's where Menendez is most likely hiding out."

"Just because Serena's brother, the plastic surgeon, was killed in Spain, that doesn't mean Menendez is still around."

"I think he is. Menendez is Latin American, so he'd fit in very easily. Not just culturally, either. Forty percent of Europe's drug trade comes in through Spain, which is only a short boat ride from Morocco. So it's also a good place for Menendez to stay on top of his global narcotics operation. That, more than anything, would be his biggest incentive for choosing Spain as his new base of operations."

"You make a good point. I didn't know you were so well-informed about the statistics of the European drug trade."

"Crime is my business. I try to keep up."

Nick walked toward the tunnel, but Kate stopped him, tugging on his sleeve.

"We're not going back through there," Kate said. "We'll go down to the plaza and take Rua do Alecrim back up."

"That's disappointing," Nick said. "I was hoping to see you in action again. It's kind of sexy in a violent, perverted sort of way."

"Gosh, knowing that makes my day complete."

"I thought you'd want me to be open about my feelings now that we're married."

"We're not married, and if you don't behave, I'll tell my father on you."

They were nearly at the foot of Rua do Alecrim when Tattoo stepped out in front of them from the shadows. He held a hatchet in each hand, the handles duct-taped to his wrists. He would have looked truly terrifying if not for the scarf wrapped under his chin and tied in a knot at the top of his head to keep his jaw from moving. The two ends of the scarf stuck out of the knot like droopy rabbit ears.

Kate sighed. "You really don't want to do this," she said to Tattoo.

Two more men appeared on either side of Tattoo from the cross street. They were the other thugs from the fight. They each had a butcher knife taped in their right hands.

Kate thought taping the butcher knives to their hands wouldn't do them much good when she broke their wrists with her baton. Then it would be just her and Nick against a guy with a broken jaw and two hatchets. So Kate felt pretty good about her odds.

She heard a shuffle of feet behind her and knew more men had joined the party.

"What have we got behind us?" she asked Nick, while she kept her eyes on the hatchet guy.

"A big ugly guy with an ice pick, and a moron with a steak knife."

Kate flicked her baton open.

"I suppose you're unarmed?" she said to Nick.

"You suppose correct."

Someone gave a shrill whistle from the vicinity of the tunnel, capturing everyone's attention, and Jake O'Hare emerged from the darkness with one hand behind his back.

"I think you should leave this nice couple alone," he said to the thugs. "Or you'll have to deal with me."

Icepick laughed. "What are you going to do about it, old man?"

Jake brought his hand out from behind his back. "I'll shoot you with this flare gun, and then I'll kill the guy next to you while he's still wiping your brains out of his eyes."

Billy Dee Snipes stepped out of the shadows behind Tattoo, swung his machete at Tattoo's head, and sliced off the knot that held the scarf in place. Tattoo's broken jaw dropped, he screamed in agony, and reached for his face. Unfortunately, with two hatchets taped to his hands, he chopped off half his right ear before he realized his mistake.

Whoosh! Billy Dee sliced the air in front of him with his machete. "The next swing takes off somebody's head. Do you still want to play?"

The four thugs ran off like cockroaches exposed to the light, leaving Tattoo behind in his sad and painful predicament.

Jake watched as Tattoo staggered past him and went whimpering toward the tunnel. "What kind of idiot tapes hatchets to both his hands?"

"Someone who thinks a tattoo of a dead goat on his head is stylish," Nick said. "Did you two follow us here?"

"No," Jake said. "We were just out looking for a drink."

"In this neighborhood?" Kate asked.

Jake looked around. "What's wrong with it?"

Kate gestured to the tunnel with her baton. "Guys like that."

"So we met some of the colorful locals. It's what gives a place charm."

"Charm?" Kate said. "They had knives and axes."

Jake shrugged. "Billy Dee has a machete, and he is very charming."

"This is true," Billy Dee said.

"I think you guessed that we were here to see Diogo Alves and you wanted to make sure we came out alive," Kate said.

"You can handle yourself just fine," Jake said and shifted his gaze to Nick. "You, I am not so sure about."

"I'm more dangerous than I look," Nick said. "But I appreciate you both showing up, regardless of why it happened."

"Me, too." Kate bent down, closed her baton against the

pavement, and returned it to her pocket. "And now I'm going back to my luxurious suite. I have big plans for the rest of the evening."

"That sounds promising," Nick said. "What did you have in mind?"

"Room service," Kate said.

16

Nick tossed his keys onto the sideboard in the small foyer, then locked and bolted the door to the suite.

"Honey, I'm home," he yelled.

It was nine at night and Kate was on the couch with her iPad. She was barefoot, wearing a too-big T-shirt and gray sweatpants. "Why do you always yell when you come in?"

"I don't want to surprise you and get shot or garroted or whacked with your baton because you think I'm an intruder."

"You *are* an intruder," Kate said. "You're intruding on my peace and quiet. When is something going to happen? I'm going goofy sitting here with nothing to do. It's been three days."

"You could be a tourist."

"I did that."

"You could get some exercise."

"I did that, too," Kate said.

"We could pretend we're actually married," Nick said.

"I don't think so."

"What have you got against marriage?"

"It's not marriage. It's *you*! You have no respect for the law."

"I respect some laws."

"You're on the FBI's Most Wanted list. What kind of a future would we have? What would I tell the children?"

Nick went to the refreshment center and poured himself a whiskey. "We're talking about a *pretend* marriage, right?"

"Of course."

"With a pretend future and pretend kids?"

"I might have gotten carried away."

Nick took his drink to the couch and sat next to Kate. He took a sip of the whiskey and smiled.

"What's with the smile?" Kate asked.

"I'm enjoying myself. Good whiskey. Nice room. My pretend wife snuggled next to me."

"I'm not snuggled."

Nick slid his arm around her and cuddled her into him. "Now you are."

"Don't get any ideas," Kate said.

"Too late. I have lots of ideas. Would you like to hear some of them?"

"No!"

"Where's your sense of adventure? What about bravery?"

"What about reckless stupidity?"

Nick gave her a squeeze and took another sip of the whiskey. "I heard back from my contacts in Berlin and Paris today. They had names of potential buyers, but none of the names were on the chocolate list."

"So we're left with Alves."

"I have some other lines out there, but Alves is the most likely to help us." He glanced down at her iPad. "What are you looking at?"

"Rodney Smoot sent us some stills taken from the underwater footage of the golden table and piles of coins. They're peeking out from the silt and are totally convincing. There's nothing about them that would indicate they're digital creations."

The shipping container that held the render farm computers was delivered on the afternoon of the fourth day Nick and Kate were in Lisbon. An hour later Nick got a message that Diogo Alves wanted to meet at the University of Lisbon's Institute of Anatomy.

The institute was in an old building that smelled of age and medicine, of dust, rubbing alcohol, and formaldehyde. Nick and Kate walked down a long, empty hall to the last room on the floor.

They found Diogo Alves sitting on a stool in the center of the small room, surrounded by thousands of jars of human organs and body parts floating in liquid. The jars filled glass cabinets and covered all the tables and counters. There were even some on the floors. Shafts of sunshine from the barely open shutters refracted through the prisms of the glass jars and liquids to make the organs glow with an eerie supernatural vibrancy.

"What is this place?" Kate asked.

"For centuries, scientists have been saving human body parts to study," Alves said to Nick and Kate. "This is a collection that showcases the many different methods of anatomical preservation. What the scientists chose to save, and how they did it, is even more interesting than the organs." Alves sat back and held his hand out to the jar directly in front of him. "Allow me to introduce my great-great-great-great-grandfather and namesake, Diogo Alves."

The jar contained a perfectly preserved human head, its face pressed up so close to the glass that it appeared to be kissing it. The resemblance between the living Alves and the head in the jar was uncanny. The living Alves might as well have been looking at his own reflection in a mirror instead of at a head in a jar.

"How often do you come here?" Nick asked Alves.

"At least once or twice a week, usually more. How many men do you know who can visit with one of their forefathers?"

The disembodied head was wide-eyed with a look of surprise.

"He looks like he wasn't expecting to die," Kate said.

"I like to think he was seeing beyond," Alves said. "I cherish this opportunity to spend time with him. I come here to get Diogo's advice on things. He's a very wise man."

"He talks to you," Kate said.

"Diogo doesn't speak to me directly, of course. But yes, I hear him, the way some people I suppose hear God speaking to them. Sometimes I could swear he's actually looking at me, that his eyes follow me as I move around the room."

Kate was sure if she stared at the head long enough, she'd think the eyes were following her, too. And then she'd get sick and throw up.

"You should be honored that I invited you here to share this intimacy with me," Alves said.

"I certainly am," Nick said. "I know that allowing us to be here with you means that you take us, and our business relationship, very seriously."

"Thank you, Nick. The people I contacted on your behalf entertained your proposal because they have personal relationships with me. If you have misled me, and cheat these people in any way, they will blame me for it. And then I will seek Diogo's advice on how to deal with you." Alves gestured to the jar. "My ancestor is not a forgiving or merciful man. Some of these jars contain recent donations to the collection from people who have disappointed me."

Kate couldn't help but glance at the nearest jar. A big floating eyeball stared back at her. She knew the chance to deliver this threat was the real reason Alves had summoned them here.

"Don't worry," Kate said. "We're all going to get very rich from this. Nobody is going to be disappointed."

"I hope so." Alves reached into his breast pocket and handed Nick a slip of paper. "Here are three names. If you wish to contact them, I will make the arrangements. My commission will be deducted before you receive any funds."

"Works for me," Nick said.

"Let me and Diogo give you a piece of advice. Think very carefully before you take the next step," Alves said. "These are not men who suffer fools. But they do enjoy making fools suffer."

Nick and Kate returned to the ship, booted up Kate's MacBook at a table in the mess hall, and ran the three names that Alves had given them against Ryerson's list of chocolate customers. One name was common to both lists. Demetrio Violante.

"I'm not surprised," Nick said, sitting across the table from her.

"You know him?"

"I know *about* him. The same is true for every person who was suggested to us. I've sized them all up for fleecing at one time or another."

"I didn't know it was such a small world."

"The kind of person who has tens of millions of dollars to play with and is still greedy enough to take outrageous risks to acquire even more money is also the perfect mark for me."

"*Was*," Kate said. "You aren't swindling people anymore. What kind of hustle were you thinking about running on Violante?"

"A real estate scam," Nick said. "I considered selling him a resort development that's a ghost town now near Puerto Banús. The financing collapsed and it was abandoned when it was half-completed."

"But you don't own the land."

"I don't let insignificant details like that concern me."

"What made you think Violante would be interested in the property?"

"He showed up in Marbella a few years ago with lots of cash, ambition, and good luck. Within a few days of his arrival, he managed to buy one of the biggest and most successful construction companies in the Costa del Sol for next to nothing."

"How did he manage that?"

"The founding partner of the firm accidentally set himself on fire at a Marbella gas station and blew the place up."

"That's an unusual accident."

"The police say he lit a cigar while filling up the tank on his Bentley, which was odd, because he didn't smoke. The gas station, which was completely destroyed in the massive explosion, happened to be on a key piece of property that the construction company needed to build a condo complex. But the owner's stubborn refusal to sell had forced them to scuttle the project."

"Let me guess. After the 'accident,' the remaining partners in the construction company suddenly decided to retire and the gas station owner sold the property."

Nick nodded. "And the detective who investigated the death and determined that it was a tragic accident later moved into one of the new condos. It's funny how things just manage to work out for some people."

"Hilarious," Kate said. "Let's see what Lester Menendez looks like now that he's Demetrio Violante."

"You won't find any photos. Violante doesn't allow his picture to be taken. He's very concerned about his privacy."

"I'm sure he is," Kate said. "Even with a new face and body. Where does he live?"

"On a peak outside of Marbella. It's like a fortress. The only way to access it is from a private road or by air. He has a completely unobstructed 360-degree view from his property. He can see all the way to Africa. There's no way to reach his place without him seeing you coming."

"Which means he's probably got a secret escape tunnel."

"Who doesn't?"

"If you knew so much about Violante, how come you weren't aware of his passion for chocolate?"

"There were a lot of things I didn't know about him. For instance, I wasn't aware that he was actually one of the most powerful and sadistic drug lords on earth."

"Would knowing that have made you scrap the con you were thinking about?"

"The risk might have made it even more enticing to me. But the point is, I only knew the big picture. I would have learned the small details before mounting the con."

"More than what we know going into this one?"

"A lot more," he said.

"Doesn't that scare you?"

"I'm protected by an ex–Navy commando, a retired pirate with a razor-sharp machete, and a senior citizen with a garrote in his underwear," he said. "Why would I be afraid of anything?"

Reyna was naked and supple, with smooth, natural curves, a flat stomach, and long legs that she leisurely kicked, propelling her firm body across the lap pool. Her string bikini bottoms were draped carelessly over the arm of a patio chair and her ever-present AK-47 was propped against it.

Demetrio Violante sat in a silk bathrobe on his balcony, watching his bodyguard swim while he snacked on black chocolate truffles filled with champagne and flecked with twenty-four-karat gold flakes. The chocolate was delicious, and it pleased him to know that he was so rich that he crapped gold.

From where he sat, he could look out over his lushly landscaped hilltop property to the whitewashed walls and terra-cotta rooftops of Marbella, to the peak of Gibraltar, and to the shores of North Africa across the Mediterranean Sea. Spectacular vistas, Violante thought, but not as spectacular as Reyna.

He watched her leave the pool and stretch out on a chaise longue. He liked to look at her. It was part of their foreplay. He studied her strong cheekbones, and her lips. It was a face shaped by evolution and DNA, not by implants and a scalpel. He especially appreciated that because he was now sewn into an uncomfortable costume of flesh.

In less than an hour Violante's driver would deliver the Hartleys. He hoped the Hartleys were the real deal because he was bored. He needed a new adventure. Acquiring the *Santa Isabel* treasure was especially appealing. He knew every detail of the shipwreck. He'd been obsessed with it as a child. Of course, there was no way he was going to pay the Hartleys the millions they wanted. Nor would he let anyone live who knew that the astonishing fortune had been found. The Hartleys, their crew, and even Alves would all have to die, but only after he'd made sure they hadn't told anybody else about the gold. That part would appeal to Reyna. She was really a delightfully sick young woman.

17

Nick and Kate were driven into Marbella by Violante's chauffeur in an S-Class Mercedes along the aptly named Golden Mile. The boulevard was lined with ocean-view mansions and led into a shopping district filled with famous names such as Versace, Gucci, and Louis Vuitton. The streets were clogged with Ferraris, Rolls-Royces, Lamborghinis, Bentleys, and BMWs.

The driver steered them out of the city and headed north on the A-376 up into the Sierra Blanca hills. It wasn't long before the housing developments thinned out and the only homes left were widely spaced modern-day castles on private hilltops separated from their neighbors by deep gorges.

They turned off the highway onto a winding single-lane strip of asphalt that climbed steeply, and precariously, up the hill. The road ended at a large iron gate set into a high stone wall with cameras mounted on the top and a small security booth out front, manned by an armed guard.

The guard peered in to look at the driver, gave Kate and Nick a quick once-over, and waved them through. The gate yawned open onto a cobblestoned driveway that cut through lush tropical landscaping and led into a courtyard ringed by eight garages. An elaborate fountain with a sculpture of Neptune holding a trident was in the center of the courtyard.

The sprawling two-story house was typical Spanish Mediterranean, with brilliant white stucco walls and brown-orange terra-cotta tiles on the roof. The exterior architecture included lots of arches, elaborate wrought-iron railings, rounded pillars, awnings, and balconies of all sizes, all adorned with overflowing flower boxes. It was a surprisingly floral touch for a bloodthirsty killer.

Kate noted the large satellite dish on the roof. She doubted it was used for watching ESPN and pay-per-view movies. It was large enough to contact extraterrestrial life.

Violante was waiting on the front steps to greet them. He was tall and slightly pudgy, and dressed in a loose white linen shirt and slacks. His wet, slicked-back, artificially brown hair had an unnaturally orange tint that matched the terra-cotta tiles. His tight, plasticized face looked to Kate more like a computer-generated videogame character than an actual human being.

"Thank you for coming to Marbella. I am Demetrio Violante." He gestured to the woman standing beside him. "And this is Reyna Socorro, my head of security."

174

Reyna's pixie-cut hair was platinum blond, and contrasted sharply with her pitch-black eyebrows and deeply tanned skin. She was also dressed in white linen, with an AK-47 slung over her shoulder as casually as a purse. Kate could tell from the way Reyna's flinty eyes studied them that the rifle wasn't a fashion statement. This woman was a killer.

"You've got nothing to fear from us," Nick said, shaking Violante's outstretched hand. "We're harmless archaeologists bearing gifts."

"You can never tell," Reyna said, looking at Kate. "It's the ones who appear harmless who are often the most danger- ous."

"Thank you for sending the car to pick us up," Kate said, though she knew they'd done it more as a security precaution than as a courtesy. They wanted to control how and when their guests arrived. "It was very kind of you."

"We know we can be hard to find," Violante said. "Intentionally so, to be honest. Please come inside."

They followed him into a grand two-story gallery filled with natural light that flowed from overhead skylights, down through a transparent Plexiglas floor. A lap pool ran under the floor like a river, through the house and out into the garden. More light spilled in through the gallery's huge windows, inten- sifying the effect of the white-on-white furniture.

Kate squinted against the glare and thought it would be a miracle if everyone in the house didn't have cataracts.

To the left of the gallery was a book-lined study, and a guest bathroom, the door ajar just enough so Kate could see it was larger than her sister's kitchen.

"I thought you might enjoy something sweet while we talk," Violante said, leading them across the gallery.

The gallery opened to an outdoor living room that overlooked the Mediterranean. It was an unusually large covered balcony with overhead fans and comfortable white-on-white cushioned wicker furniture. A table in the center of the room was piled high with a huge selection of gold-flecked and gold-covered chocolates arranged around bowls of fresh fruit and a burbling chocolate fountain. It was the most amazing display of chocolate Kate had ever seen. She half-expected Oompa Loompas to come dancing out to introduce it.

Kate carefully selected one of the gold-flaked chocolates. "I assume these are edible?"

"Of course." Violante demonstrated by popping one of the smaller golden chocolates into his mouth. "The flakes are pure twenty-four-karat gold and biologically inert."

Nick chose a truffle and admired it as if it were jewelry. "Why would you want to eat something so valuable?"

"Don't let the glitter fool you," Violante said. "The chocolate is far more valuable than the gold coating it. Each piece is seventy-five percent pure dark chocolate, made with scarce single-origin cacao from private plantations in Madagascar, Chile, Côte d'Ivoire, Trinidad, or Ecuador."

"You really didn't have to do this for us," Nick said.

"On the contrary," Violante said. "A treasure in golden

chocolate seemed only fitting to celebrate and honor your discovery of the *Santa Isabel*."

"These chocolates are fabulous," Kate said. "But they would look even better on golden dishes on a one-ton solid gold table."

Violante nodded. "I agree."

Nick handed Violante a picture of the table that Rodney had digitally created. The table was half-buried in silt and covered with concretions. It still looked magnificent.

"This would be treasure enough on its own," Nick said, "but the seafloor is covered with gold dishes and piles of coins. It's a spectacular sight."

A second picture showed gold coins and dishes strewn across the ocean floor, covering rocks, peeking through silt, wedged between bits of coral.

"How did you find it?" Violante asked.

Nick reached for another chocolate. "Years of research going through historical records, old maps, logbooks kept by sailors on other ships who saw the sinking, descriptions of the stars in the sky, that sort of thing. Boring, academic detective work. Then it came down to instinct and technology. We spent months at sea in the area where we thought the *Santa Isabel* had gone down. We dragged sonar equipment behind our ship and mapped the seafloor, looking for telltale anomalies. We were in our eighth fruitless month, our money and morale critically low, when we passed over this vast, abyssal plane. That's when we started to see huge sonar spikes that didn't look like rocks."

"What did they look like?"

"Cannons," Kate said. "So we dropped our ROV, an unmanned sub loaded with cameras and things, into the water and sent it to the bottom for a look. We found the cannons, and a whole lot more."

"How deep down is the treasure?"

"About twelve hundred feet," Nick said. "It's not going to be an easy salvage, particularly if you don't want to attract any attention while you're doing it."

Violante waved off the concern. "Blindness is easy to buy."

"If you have the power and the resources," Nick said. "You do, we don't. That's why we're here. You can't imagine how infuriating it is for us to find one of the greatest treasures in the history of mankind and not be able to keep it all for ourselves."

"Coming to you is our way of at least getting something out of it," Kate said.

Violante's face was a frozen mask and eerily devoid of expression. "Seventeen and a half million dollars is more than something."

"It is if you take that amount out of context," Nick said. "But given the cash value, rarity, and historical significance of what you're getting in return, it's a pittance. Your treasure will make England's crown jewels look like costume jewelry by comparison."

"Not that anyone will know you have it to make that comparison," Kate said, helping herself to another chocolate. "Except us."

"And your crew," Reyna said.

"We'll take care of them from the money you pay us," Nick said.

"By the time we've paid Alves and everyone else their share," Kate said, "we'll be lucky if we can walk away with a measly ten or eleven million."

"You could be lucky if you walk away at all," Violante said.

Kate smiled at him. "You mean, what's to stop you from beating the location of the *Santa Isabel* out of us right now?"

"If I was that sort of person," he said.

"Thankfully, you're a civilized gentleman," Nick said. "But like Reyna said, you can never tell, so we've taken precautions. The wreck is mined with explosives. If the two of us don't return unharmed in the next eight hours, our crew will blow it up."

"So what?" Reyna said. "The gold will still be there."

"Over a much wider area and in particles so small, you'd have to sift them out of the sand," Nick said.

"It would take you months, and cost you millions of dollars, just to end up with the same amount of gold you've got right here decorating your candy. Hardly worth the effort. It would be much cheaper just to pay us."

Violante dipped an apple slice into the chocolate and took a bite as he leisurely considered what they'd said.

"You tell an interesting story, but that's all it is," he said. "You could be a couple of daring con artists. The coins could have come from a previously salvaged shipwreck and these photographs could be fakes. I will have to see the *Santa Isabel* for myself before I give you any money."

"Your concerns are entirely understandable," Nick said. "But at the same time, we have to protect the location of the shipwreck from being discovered or we have nothing to sell. If you'd like us to take you out to it, you'll have to let us search you for any communications or tracking devices, confine you to a windowless room during the voyage, and do whatever else is necessary to prevent you from learning exactly where you are."

"You'd be treating me like a prisoner," Violante said.

"Or a kidnapping victim," Reyna said. "This could be a clever trick to get you to hand yourself to people who intend to ransom you for your fortune. If you survived, you'd be ridiculed for the rest of your life as the dumbest kidnapping victim ever."

"Reyna is right. Wealthy individuals like me are frequently kidnapped, and exorbitant ransoms are quietly paid. It's all kept out of the media, of course. But it's a fact of life," Violante said. "I live on a mountaintop and surround myself with Reyna and armed security guards to prevent it from happening to me. It would be absurd if I simply handed myself over to you without any protection or guarantees."

"Makes sense," Nick said. "What sort of guarantee do you have in mind?"

Reyna selected a strawberry, dipped it in chocolate, licked the chocolate off the strawberry, and ate the strawberry.

"I'll keep your wife," Reyna said with one last seductive swipe of her tongue across her lower lip.

Nick was silent for a beat. "What makes you so sure I

wouldn't sacrifice her for a huge ransom and a shot at the high life as a single man?" he said to Reyna.

"Because I'd find you, drag you back here, and cut your wife into pieces with a chainsaw while you watched," Reyna said. "And then I'd serve her to you grilled, with a touch of salt and olive oil, as your last meal before I cut you up and ate you myself."

"That's a very vivid and gruesome threat," Nick said. "You wouldn't really do that, would you?"

"Let's hope we don't have to find out," Reyna said and smiled at Kate.

Nick and Kate Hartley accepted the terms, and Violante agreed to meet them in three days at a dock in Málaga for the exchange. He'd get on the boat with Nick, and Kate would stay with Reyna.

The Hartleys got into the Mercedes, and Violante's man drove them back to the airport.

"They might be very good treasure hunters but they are inept at business," Violante said to Reyna. "The fools think they will be safe once I've paid them. People that stupid deserve to die."

"You're right," Reyna said. "But the woman is dangerous."

"You can tell that just by looking at her?"

"It's what you pay me for."

"It's one of many things," Violante said. "But how dangerous could an archaeologist be?"

"I don't know if she's an archaeologist. I saw how she looked at me and carried herself. She's a coiled venomous snake, ready to strike."

"Then it's a good thing that she's the one staying here with you. I'm sure you two will have lots of fun together. It's a shame that I won't be able to participate."

"I can find us a woman for tonight."

"It won't be quite the same," he said with a sigh. "But go ahead. We'll try to make do."

Willie was waiting for Nick and Kate at the Málaga–Costa del Sol Airport on a private plane they'd "borrowed" in Lisbon for the one-and-a-half-hour flight. It wasn't until they were in the air that Nick and Kate finally felt safe to talk about their encounter with Violante.

"That went well," Nick said.

"How do you figure?"

"We weren't tortured, and he agreed to go out with us on the boat."

"But I'm going to be their hostage."

"In a hilltop palace, eating expensive chocolates, taking swims and getting a tan."

"With creepy Reyna watching my every move."

"She really knows how to eat a strawberry," Nick said. "How come you don't eat fruit like that?"

"Fruit is not my thing," Kate said. "Watch me eat an In-N-Out burger sometime."

"Something to add to my bucket list," Nick said.

"What bothers me is that I am going to be stuck up there while you and seven civilians are at sea with a brutal drug lord."

"Those seven civilians aren't exactly harmless. Your father scares the bejeezus out of me."

Kate smiled. It was true. Her father could be a scary guy.

18

While Nick and Kate were away in Marbella, Rodney Smoot was busy setting up the render farm computers. He was in the cargo hold, eating dinner with Jake and Billy Dee, when Kate and Nick came on board. Jake and Billy Dee were eating peanut butter and jelly sandwiches. Rodney was eating a micro-waved Hot Pocket Philly Steak and Cheese.

"They sell Hot Pockets in Lisbon?" Kate asked.

"I have no idea," Rodney said. "I packed a suitcase full of them to play it safe. I couldn't take the chance that they don't have them here. It's my brain fuel."

"You're in Lisbon," Nick said. "You should be treating your brain to *Pastéis de bacalhau.*"

"What's that?" Rodney asked.

"Salt cod cakes," Nick said.

"That's revolting," Rodney said.

"What if I told you that the cod comes frozen from Norway, so it's essentially a defrosted meal?" Nick asked.

"I might try it in a Hot Pocket," Rodney said. "With the garlic butter crust."

"I'd go with the pretzel crust," Kate said.

"Smart choice," Jake said. "You can't go wrong with pretzels, and maybe you could add bacon."

Nick studied the exterior of the shipping container that held the computers. There were cables strung between the container and the walls of the cargo hold. The cables would supply the computers and their cooling system with power and relay the data stream up to the command center.

Nick peered inside the container. The banks of computers hummed, and he could hear a fan pumping in cool air.

"How's the setup of the render farm going?" he asked Rodney. "I'm no expert, but it looks to me like you're in good shape."

"Give me an hour and another Hot Pocket, and we'll be ready for a test drive," Rodney said.

"Great, because we're setting sail tomorrow," Nick said.

An hour later, Kate met Nick in the corridor. They were both on their way to the remotely operated vehicle command center.

"I just did some research on Reyna Socorro," Kate said. "Menendez's cartel recruited her from FARC, the Colombian rebels who've been funding their revolution against the state with kidnapping, extortion, and drug dealing. She was the leader of a guerrilla cell that specialized in kidnapping politicians, soldiers, police officers, and foreign nationals. They'd be chained and held hostage in the jungle for years for ransom, used as human shields and to sow fear among the cartel's enemies."

"No wonder she was so quick to see this con as a kidnapping scheme instead of what it really is. That's good for us."

"She's the one who suggested taking me hostage," Kate said.

"Exactly. She's fixated on kidnappings. So she won't see what's really going on and neither will Violante."

"When FARC leaders told her they wanted to generate some positive publicity by releasing two police officers that she'd held hostage for three years, she executed the prisoners instead and walked out of the jungle with her AK-47 to join the Menendez cartel."

"I don't think it's the same AK-47," said Nick.

"You're missing the point."

"She's a badass, I get it. So is her boss. That's why we are taking them down, isn't it?"

"Reyna doesn't follow orders well," Kate said. "You should expect a double-cross. She could decide to not give me back, or to hurt me a bit, just to test how serious you really are."

"Then she'd be making a big mistake."

"Because you think you can convince her that you'd kill Violante and blow up the gold if I'm harmed?"

"Because she doesn't know what a badass *you* are."

They walked into the command center, where Boyd, Willie,

and Tom were all waiting. Boyd was in uniform and wearing his eye patch. The command center was dark inside to accentuate the lit-up buttons on the console and the meaningless data scrolling on the monitors.

Nick whistled with approval. "Nicely done, Tom."

"Tom has genuine theatrical flair," Boyd said. "This room has character and drama. It's as if Tom is an actor whose instrument is a hammer and nails."

"Thank you, Boyd," Tom said.

"Captain Bridger," Boyd said. "And I believe a salute is in order."

Tom gave him the finger, and Boyd, staying in character, returned the salute.

Nick pulled out the chair in front of the ROV joystick and sat down. The screen in front of him was black. Tom leaned over his shoulder to point out how the joysticks worked.

"The center joystick controls the movement of the ROV. The two smaller ones control the left and right robotic arms."

"Seems simple enough."

"What do the buttons on the joysticks do?" Kate asked.

"Nothing," Tom said. "They're decoration."

Willie stepped closer to examine the controls for herself. "How fast does it go?"

"It doesn't go at all," Nick said. "The ROV is still on deck. This is basically a videogame."

"It better not look like one," Kate said.

"We're about to find out, Miss Optimism," Nick said. "On

second thought, let's have the biggest skeptic on board take the test drive." He got out of the chair and offered it to Kate. "You do it."

Kate sat down and put her hand on the center joystick. "Okay, ready."

"Not quite," Nick said, taking two tiny flesh-colored earbuds from his pocket. He slipped one into his ear and handed the other to Kate. It was the same communications device the entire team would be using when the con was live. Rodney had one, too, as did Jake and Billy Dee, who were in the cargo hold with him. "Can you hear me, Rodney?"

In the cargo hold, Rodney stood at a keyboard inside the open shipping container and faced a screen that would show him whatever Nick saw on the bridge screen. Jake and Billy Dee were beside Rodney, but their attention was on another screen, showing the view from a surveillance camera in the command center. Their job would be to keep tabs on what the "driver" of the ROV was doing.

"I hear you loud and clear," Rodney said to Nick. "Press the blue button beside your joystick, Kate, and off we go."

Kate pressed the button and the murky, emerald depths in front of the ROV appeared on the screen.

"It's awfully dark," Kate said. "I can't see anything."

"Turn on the ROV's lights," Rodney said.

Kate searched for a button marked LIGHTS on the console and pressed it.

The flood lamps atop the ROV flashed on, illuminating the

nose and outstretched arms of the vehicle and several yards of the ocean floor ahead of it. Startled fish darted out of sight. A crab scrambled between two rocks. Some kelp swayed in the current. The picture was as clear as it could be in deep, silty water. Kate pushed the joystick forward and the ROV slowly cruised along over the seabed.

"The crab was a clever touch," Nick said.

"I was afraid it might break into song," Kate said.

"It's the details you take for granted, like the particles floating in the water or the coral on the rocks, that count the most and are the hardest things to get right in effects shots," Rodney said. "You'll only notice them if they look fake to you. If you don't notice them, and are able to focus on the crab, it means that you're already convinced, at least on an unconscious level, that the environment you're seeing is real. So now you're going to be much more willing to believe in a fortune in gold when you see it."

"It's the same with any con," Nick said. "The real trick is being prepared for the mark to do the unexpected."

Nick grabbed the joystick from Kate and jerked it hard to the right. The ROV made a sharp turn. The sudden motion of the ROV kicked up silt on the ocean floor, made the kelp sway, and scattered fish. It also revealed large rocks scattered ahead along a different stretch of the seabed.

Rodney laughed. "Nice try. If you thought you'd startle the computer, that it wouldn't be ready for you, think again. You're not going to surprise it and find a corner of the ocean missing, or cause the computer to lock up while it renders the new setting."

"I was more interested in seeing how the things around the ROV reacted to sudden movement," Nick said. "It didn't all stay still."

"Of course not," Rodney said. "It's a fully reactive ecosystem."

Kate pushed the joystick forward and scraped the underside of the ROV over a large rock, making the camera shudder, and the lights wobble.

"The ROV is reactive to the environment, too," Rodney said. "As you can see."

"Do you want me to drive?" Willie asked Kate.

"I did it on purpose."

"Sure you did. You're going to destroy a very expensive piece of equipment before our guy even gets here."

"It's not real," Kate said. "And even if I do trash it, it's not like this video has a memory."

"Actually, it does," Rodney said. "If you pick up an item from the ocean floor on one foray, you don't want it to still be there when you come back again later. But we'll erase the memory of this session and start fresh next time."

"So where's the *Santa Isabel's* debris field?" Kate asked.

"Check the sonar map," Nick said, tapping another, smaller monitor to the left of the main screen.

The monitor was like the GPS navigation screen in a car. It showed a graphic representation of the ocean floor topography and a black arrowhead moving across it.

"Think of this as your underwater navigation system," Rodney said. "It's tracking your movements across the ocean floor. The debris field is the red area to the north."

Kate steered the ROV along the bottom, over a field of sand and jagged rocks, until a glimmer to the right caught her eye.

"What have we here?" Kate turned the ROV toward the glimmer, caused by the light reflecting off something in a pile of stones. And as she got closer, there were more sparkles on the pile, which she now saw wasn't made of stones at all. It was actually hundreds of spilled gold coins, caked with concretions. "We're rich."

"Not until we get the coins to the surface and cash them in," Nick said. "Let's take a sample."

Kate spent the next hour using the ROV's robotic arms to scoop up the gold and dump it into a bucket. She was impressed and relieved that it all worked, and she declared the operation good to go.

The entire crew met one more time to go over the choreography of the con, how it would all go down from the moment Demetrio Violante stepped on board until the moment when he left the ship again.

Kate went back to her cabin and contacted Jessup to ask him to have one of his CIA buddies deliver a particular piece of bugging technology to her at one of their dead drops, a place for passing messages to undercover or double agents, in Lisbon.

The dead drop was a hollow brick on the grounds of Castelo de São Jorge above the Alfama. Kate retrieved the tiny device, about the size of a thumb drive, that same night with Jake as her backup. Afterward they had a father-daughter dinner at a mom-and-pop café tucked away in one of the twisting streets down the hill from the castle.

They sat at one of the three tables and ate grilled sardines and diced pork covered with clams while the owners, and two local patrons, watched a Portuguese soap opera on the TV mounted on the wall.

"This is nice," Jake said. "I wish we'd been able to do this more often when you were growing up."

"Mounting international cons to capture fugitive drug lords?"

"Family dinners. Every time I was stuck in some wet, mosquito-infested jungle, crouched in the mud eating my K rations, I thought about what I was missing back home."

"You loved it. You still do. That's why you're here."

"I loved you and Megan," he said. "I'm not sure I showed that enough. *That's* why I'm here and that's why I live with her."

Kate reached out and squeezed his hand. "You have nothing to apologize for. You were a great dad then and you are now. You were a single father in the military. You did the best that you possibly could for us. Megan and I both know that. So give yourself a break."

"You're telling me I should just shut up and enjoy this."

"Yeah. As much as possible considering we've got clams on our pork. I know I'm supposed to be loving all the local color, and I sort of like Portuguese soap operas even though I haven't a clue what they're saying, but this meal would be a lot better if everything was breaded and deep fried."

"Next time I'll Google a Popeyes."

19

Willie steered the *Seaquest* away from the dock and down the Rio Tejo. It was the biggest vessel she'd ever piloted, and Kate was at high alert on the bridge with her.

"Relax," Willie said. "Our top speed is twelve knots, lumbering at best. How much damage can I do?"

"There are a lot of small boats out there," Kate said. "You could run over one of them."

"If they can't see me coming and get out of the way, good riddance."

Kate knew it was gallows bravado. Willie for the most part had good instincts, and she was aided by Billy Dee at the bow and Jake on the bridge. Jake watched the radar, sonar, and GPS, keeping them in the channel and headed in the right direction.

Málaga was 254 nautical miles from Lisbon. The *Seaquest* could have made it there in a day at top speed, but they took it slow along the Portuguese coast and through the Strait of Gibraltar, arriving at the port in a day and a half. As soon as they docked, Nick reminded everyone to assume that they were under constant surveillance by Violante's people.

"The Hartleys and their research vessel have arrived in Málaga," Reyna told Violante.

Violante was in his office, keeping tabs via satellite on the flow of drugs and money through his global criminal empire. His eyes were locked on three screens that showed the email communications between his people, a running tally of the money moving into and out of his accounts, and a map indicating the positions of each of the airplanes, boats, trucks, trains, and cars that were smuggling his drugs.

"I want their boat and every crew member watched at all times," he said. "I want to know what they do and who they see."

"They aren't doing much. They're just restocking their supplies. We're looking for opportunities to slip tracking devices into whatever they bring back on board . . . including you."

"You're not putting a tracking device up my ass," Violante said.

"It might be fun."

"It wasn't last time you tried it."

"It's an acquired pleasure," Reyna said.

"So far I haven't acquired it."

"Very well, we'll make sure you're covered without requiring surgery or other insertions into your body. However, along that line of thought, I'd like to torture the woman."

"I'm sure you would."

"I know I could break her while you're away."

"What if Kate lies to you just to stop the pain? What if she really doesn't know the exact location and only her husband, Nick, has the coordinates?"

"We won't release her when you return and then we'll give her back to Nick in pieces, say fingers and toes to start, until he tells us what we want to know."

"What if he's willing to sacrifice his wife for seventeen and a half million dollars?"

Reyna shrugged. "Then we really have nothing to lose by torturing her."

He looked up at her again. "How do you figure that?"

"They are both greedy and desperate. They want the money too much to walk away from the deal just because I've electrocuted her and removed a few of her fingernails. It's trading a little discomfort, or perhaps exquisite pleasure if she's wired that way, in return for lavish compensation."

"You're forgetting that there are other potential buyers," Violante said. "The Hartleys could take their offer to them."

"Not if we kill the other buyers first."

Violante sighed. "I know how much you'd enjoy torturing

Kate Hartley, and that it's been a while since your needs have been satisfied, but I don't want to take the risk. I want the treasure too much."

"That's exactly why we should take advantage of every opportunity we have to get the location of the treasure for you."

"It's premature," he said. "We don't even know if the Hartleys have really found the shipwreck."

"This is how we can find out."

"Let's do this their way for now," he said. "I'll find you someone else you can torture. There are plenty of people who possess information that I'd like to have or who simply deserve some agony. You can make a list of them while I'm gone."

The next morning, promptly at 10:00, Violante's Mercedes and a black Range Rover rolled down the wharf toward the *Seaquest* and parked at the bottom of the gangway. Nick, Kate, and Tom were on the wharf, waiting for Violante.

Four armed men in sunglasses, their black suit jackets not quite hiding their weapons, got out of the Range Rover and spread out around the Mercedes. Once the security detail was in position, Violante and Reyna got out. She was also dressed in an elegant black suit, the breeze brushing open her jacket to reveal her shoulder holster.

Violante was wearing sunglasses, a windbreaker, an untucked shirt, jeans, and running shoes. His belt had a large silver buckle.

"I didn't know how long we'd be out at sea," Violante said, "so I brought some clothes and toiletries."

His driver popped the trunk and took out a Vuitton suitcase, which he set down beside Violante.

"I want to remind you, and your security team, that you agreed to let us search you," Nick said. "And to allow us to do whatever is necessary to ensure that you won't be able to discover the location of the shipwreck during this trip."

"Be my guest." Violante raised his arms. "Pat me down."

"We're a little more high-tech than that," Nick said and nodded to Tom, who stepped forward with an electronic wand, similar to those used by the TSA. "This is designed to detect GPS chips, like those found in cellphones and iPads."

Tom began by holding the wand above Violante's head. It started beeping almost immediately. He reached for Violante's glasses, and two of the guards reflexively went for their weapons.

"Relax," Violante said to them, raising his hand to ward them off, and then he removed his glasses and gave them to Reyna. "I forgot these had a GPS chip in them. It's so she can locate me quickly if I am abducted."

"I completely understand," Nick said. "You're a wealthy man and a desirable target for kidnappers. It was a wise precaution."

Tom continued running the wand down Violante's body. It beeped again when it hit his belt buckle.

"It must be all that silver," Violante said.

"This only detects GPS signals," Tom said.

"Oh." Violante glanced at Reyna as he unbuckled his belt and pulled it out of the loops. "I didn't know about this one."

"I should have told you," Reyna said. "Again, it's for your protection. I didn't give it a second thought. My mistake."

"We all make them," Nick said.

Tom continued his sweep, crouching down to scan Violante's legs and feet. The wand beeped again over his shoes.

"Smart shoes," Violante said. "The latest thing. They track your heart rate and blood pressure when you run. It seems everything has a computer in it these days. I didn't realize there was a GPS chip in the shoe, too. What a surprise."

"It's such a high-tech world we live in," Nick said. "You never know what you'll find. There was even a tracking device in the bag of flour we bought yesterday."

"Astonishing." Violante slipped off his shoes, bent down, and handed them to his driver. He turned to Nick again. "I have an old pair of running shoes in the trunk. Dumb shoes. You can run the wand over them. Are we done now?"

"Not quite," Nick said and gestured to the boat. "One of my crew members in the bridge is holding a device that detects electromagnetic tagging particles, like the ones used by Predator drones to pinpoint targets. I don't want to alarm you or your men, but if there are any of those particles on you, which I'm sure there won't be, it will appear as if you're being painted by a sniper's targeting beam."

Before the words were even out of Nick's mouth, Violante's suitcase lit up with red dots, as did his windbreaker. It looked like an entire firing squad had him lined up in their laser sights. It clearly made Violante's security detail uncomfortable, but not the man himself.

Violante shrugged. "You can't blame a man for trying."

"You're not making it easy to establish a relationship built on trust," Nick said.

"I'm the one you're asking for seventeen and a half million dollars and who is putting himself at your mercy." Violante slipped off his windbreaker and dropped it on the suitcase. "I am the one who should be concerned about trust."

"That's why you're getting me," Kate said.

"No," Reyna said. "I am."

"I'm sure you girls will have a marvelous time together," Violante said. His driver brought him the old running shoes. Tom scanned them, and Violante slipped them on and tied the laces. He straightened and looked at Kate. "You are my guest, Mrs. Hartley. Feel free to enjoy my wine, my chocolate, and all the creature comforts of my home during your stay."

"Thank you," Kate said. "That's very generous."

"I'm afraid there aren't many creature comforts on our ship," Nick said to Violante. "But we'll try to make up for it by showing you the most spectacular treasure anyone has ever seen."

"When will you be back?" Reyna asked Nick.

"We'll give you a call when we're approaching the port," Nick said, handing Reyna a prepaid cellphone. "More than a day and less than a week."

"Remember that," Reyna said. "Because eight days from now at dawn, if I haven't heard from you, I will slit your wife's throat."

"That won't happen," Nick said.

He stepped up to Kate, slipped his arms around her, and gave her a deep, passionate kiss that sent a flash of red-hot lust curling through every part of her.

"Because you mean everything to me, I'll be back soon," Nick said to Kate.

"G-g-good," Kate said.

20

Violante glanced over his shoulder as he walked up the gangway. The Mercedes was driving off with Reyna and Kate Hartley in the backseat. The Range Rover, and his security team, remained on the wharf and would stay there until the ship left port.

He'd underestimated the Hartleys, Violante thought. He should have known that if they had the technology to find the *Santa Isabel* treasure, they would have the tools to thoroughly screen him for tracking devices. He'd made a strategic mistake and would learn from it. He'd assume that when the time came to kill the Hartleys, they would be prepared for it, not that it would save them.

His attention turned from the cars on the wharf to the ship's captain waiting to greet him on deck. The man had an eye patch, a beard, and a crisp, white uniform. Not what he'd expected to be chauffeuring this research scow. He'd expected someone more casually dressed with skin like cracked leather. This guy looked like a refugee from *The Love Boat*.

"Welcome aboard the *Seaquest*, Mr. Violante. I am Captain Bridger. Although I work for the Hartleys, I am in command of this vessel, and I will do everything in my power to make this trip a safe and enjoyable one for you."

"I appreciate that, Captain."

"I hope you will join me for dinner tonight."

"I don't have any other plans," Violante said.

"We'll be casting off now," the captain said. "Enjoy the sunshine while you can. In a few minutes, you'll be taken to your room and locked inside until dinner."

Violante had never been locked up before by anyone, and he hated the idea of it happening now. One more reason the entire crew would have to die. Nobody could know Violante had allowed himself to be held prisoner.

"I'm sure you're not happy about this, but I can sweeten the deal," Nick said to Violante. "Let me show you our pride and joy."

They walked to the bow where a robotic submarine as sleek and sexy as Violante's own Lamborghini Aventador, and about the same size, was strapped to the deck under the arm of the crane. The unmanned submarine was bright yellow with two chrome nacelles in the back and two long mechanical arms with pincers in the front. There was an array of lights along the body, spotlights on the top, and a camera housed in a sleek transparent casing on the pointed nose.

"This is our ROV," Nick said. "We lower it to the bottom of the ocean with this crane. The ROV remains attached to the ship via an armored umbilical cable that powers the vehicle and relays data back to our command center, so there's no limit to how long this baby can stay submerged. It's got a high-definition camera array as well as sonar equipment for mapping, tools that analyze the mineral content of the mud, and devices that measure water temperature and density, among other things. It's like our own version of the Mars rover."

Violante didn't need the song and dance. As soon as he saw the shiny ROV, he knew he didn't have to worry that he was the victim of an elaborate kidnapping scheme. This ROV was the real deal, and it made his heart race, because it meant the treasure was likely to be real, too.

"What does something like that ROV cost?" he asked.

"We built this ourselves to suit our needs, so it's a proprietary design," Nick said. "But ballpark is about a half a million dollars, not including the three thousand feet of tether and umbilical cable. You'll need a different sort of ROV, designed primarily for salvage, to bring the larger items up from the seabed. There are some off-the-shelf models you could buy, but it could attract attention you don't want."

Violante was beginning to realize just how complex the

salvage could be, but the challenges didn't dampen his excitement. If anything, they only increased it. "How long until we get to the shipwreck?"

Nick grinned and wagged a finger at him. "That would be telling. We might get to the shipwreck long before we inform you that we're actually there, or we might let you know right when we arrive. The bottom line is that we're not going to give you any information that could possibly help you narrow down a rough location on your own."

"I'm not that clever."

"Maybe not, but I'm sure you could hire people who are. They could make some educated guesses about where the *Santa Isabel* might be based on how long it took us to get there, the speed of our boat, the depth of the wreck, and, if we let you look out at the night sky, the positions of the stars."

"I couldn't tell one star from another."

"We won't be taking that chance," Nick said. "Speaking of which, it's time to get started."

He led Violante to the deckhouse on the stern, up a flight of stairs, and down a hall to a large cabin. There was a bunk bed, a bathroom, and a basket of chocolate bars on the writing desk. The porthole had been blacked out with paint.

"I'm sorry it's not as sumptuous as your home, but it's the best we've got," Nick said. "If you need anything, just press the call button and we'll be right down."

Violante stepped inside and immediately felt claustrophobic. "How long will I be stuck in here?"

"It's hard to say."

Nick closed the door and locked it.

Violante sat on the edge of his bed and looked at the chocolate bars in the basket. Kinder Buenos, Snickers, Milka Huesitos, M&M's, Milka Oreos, and Cadbury Tokkes. It might as well have been a basket of excrement for a man with his refined palate for chocolate.

The list of good reasons for killing the Hartleys was getting longer. He almost wished he'd given Reyna his blessing to torture the woman.

Reyna led Kate to a guesthouse on the east end of the property. The 1,400-square-foot one-bedroom bungalow was done in the same style as the main house and had a small kitchen and living room that opened out to the pool. The rear of the guesthouse overlooked a low wall and a sheer drop to the gorge below.

The front door opened into a living room with a massive flat-screen TV above the stone fireplace and an open gourmet kitchen decorated with painted tiles. Beyond that, through the open door to the master suite, Kate could see a king-size four-poster bed.

"This is very nice," Kate said, setting her gym bag on the floor by the bedroom door.

"The kitchen is fully stocked with food and wine. There are toiletries for you in the master bath and, for your entertainment, we have satellite television," Reyna said. "You also have the run of the property, of course."

"As long as I don't try to leave."

"Correct. There are cliffs on the east, west, and south sides of the estate and a high gate topped with razor wire. I've already searched your bag, and now I'm going to have to pat you down. I'm sure you understand. We don't have the sophisticated equipment here that you have on your boat."

Kate held out her arms, and Reyna slowly and carefully ran her hands along Kate's body. It was less a pat down than it was groping. The last time someone had groped Kate without an invitation, she'd broken the guy's wrist and got an honorable discharge from the Navy. Breaking Reyna's wrist wasn't an option today since Kate was playing the role of geeky, greedy archaeologist.

"All this really isn't necessary," Kate said. "I'm an archaeologist. Not Rambo."

"Of course," Reyna said, "but I would be remiss in my job if I didn't make sure you weren't hiding weapons. After you settle in you're welcome to join me for a swim. The water is relaxing."

"I think I'll jog around the property a few times to loosen up instead."

"Feel free," Reyna said.

Kate changed into a tank top, shorts, and running shoes and set off on her run around the grounds. It wasn't exercise she was after. She wanted to learn the layout of the property, determine the number of guards on patrol, and see where all the security cameras were positioned.

She circled the property four times and identified several camera blind spots, which were the result of a system that was designed to watch for attack from outside, not from within.

As she came around to the backyard for the final circuit, she saw Reyna, nude, doing laps in the pool. There were two towels out, draped over the backs of two patio chairs. One of the chairs had Reyna's AK-47 propped against it as if it were an umbrella or walking stick. Kate walked over and stood beside the rifle to catch her breath.

Reyna swam to the edge of the pool. "How was your run?" she asked Kate.

"Energizing."

"You should cool off with a swim."

"I didn't bring a suit."

"You don't need one."

"I'm bashful."

"You're afraid," Reyna said. "I don't bite. Unless asked."

Kate ignored the innuendo and casually picked up the AK-47. "Your boss isn't here, so why are you carrying this around? There's nobody to protect."

"There's you," she said.

"There's no one after me."

"Someone could try to take you away," Reyna said.

"You still think this is a plot to kidnap your boss?"

"I think you're the only leverage we have in this situation."

"So is it wise to let yourself be caught naked with your rifle out of reach?" Kate lifted the rifle and swung the barrel in Reyna's general direction.

Two red pinpoint laser dots instantly appeared dead center on Kate's chest. She looked up to see a guard on the eastern edge of the roof targeting her in the laser-guided crosshairs of his sniper rifle. She turned and saw another guard standing at the edge of the house, aiming at her with a handgun with an integrated laser sight.

"The guards like to watch me while I'm swimming," Reyna said.

"Boys will be boys." Kate carefully set the AK-47 back down against the chair.

"See you for dinner. Sevenish?" Reyna asked.

"Black tie?"

"Come as you are. We aren't formal here."

"No kidding." Kate turned and walked back toward the guesthouse. The red targeting dots stayed on her until she was well out of reach of the rifle.

Reyna remained in the pool and watched her go. She was certain Kate Hartley was dangerous. It wasn't the playacting with the gun that was the tip-off, though that had been fun. When she'd patted Kate down, she'd felt not only how toned her body was, but how her muscles tensed up in a defensive response. She knew Kate wanted to strike and was fighting the urge. Reyna found that incredibly arousing, which made the desire to torture her, with pleasure and with pain, even stronger.

She'd make another try at pleasure first, but if that failed, she didn't mind going straight to pain. One way or another, tonight Kate Hartley would be crying for mercy.

"The pirates took our ship and left me, and seventeen members of my crew, in the motorless dinghy in middle of the South China Sea," Captain Bridger said. "We'd only been adrift for an hour or so when the storm hit and the boat was capsized by an enormous wave. Two of my men drowned. They were the lucky ones."

Violante knew it was nightfall even though he hadn't been on deck. After all, he had a watch. He'd been escorted from his room and taken up a flight of stairs to the mess hall, where Captain Hollywood was waiting at a table for him. They shared a bottle of bad wine and a meal of fried chicken, green beans, and mashed potatoes. Prison food must be like this, Violante thought. Something which he'd fortunately been able to avoid.

The captain stared gravely at him with his single eye. "The sharks came after that."

"Did a shark eat your eye?" Violante asked.

"A shark isn't that dainty or selective. If one of those soulless black-eyed beasts goes for your head, he'll take it clean off," the captain said. "Like one of 'em did with poor Gilligan, a bosun's mate, who was floating right next to me. We watched Gilligan's headless body bob in his life jacket in the crimson water for hours, taunting us while the sharks circled and feasted on my crew. Seventeen men went into the water, only three came out."

Violante had lost his appetite when the repulsive plate of food had been set in front of him, but now all of Captain Cretin's talk of blood and death had restored his hunger, and he found himself digging into one of the chicken legs.

"So how did you lose your eye, Bridger?" He didn't much care, but figured a gruesome story would carry him through his side dishes.

"I'm afraid that's too painful and horrific for me to talk about."

"It must be, if it's worse than headless Gilligan and your crew getting eaten by sharks."

"You don't want to know," Nick Hartley said, sliding onto the bench beside the captain and setting down his own tray of food. "You'll have to forgive the captain. He gets morose at night after a few glasses of wine."

"Because the darkness is as pitiless as a shark's dead eyes," the captain said. "And the wine as red as man's blood on the water."

The captain picked up his tray and left.

Nick shook his head. "Sorry about that. It's not often that Captain Bridger has a fresh audience for his stories."

Violante thought he wouldn't mind stabbing his fork into the one eye Bridger had left. "No problem. I found him to be entertaining. Are we there yet?"

"You need to be patient," Nick said. "It's a virtue."

"I am not a virtuous man," Violante said.

Nick had to suppress a grin. Building up Violante's frustration was a necessary but tricky element of the con. It would make Violante's happiness more intense when he finally saw the treasure.

The con was going perfectly. The only thing Nick was worried about now was Kate.

21

After the encounter at the pool, Kate showered, dressed in a T-shirt, jeans, and running shoes, and spent the rest of the day in the guesthouse, binging on episodes of *Game of Thrones*. She ate smoked salmon, assorted cheeses, potato chips, and chocolate ice cream. It was a hostage ordeal she wouldn't share with Nick or Jessup.

At 7 P.M., she walked to the main house and went upstairs to the outdoor living room. There was an enormous seafood tower brimming over with oysters, shrimp, and crab legs in crushed ice on the same patio table where the golden chocolate had been before.

Reyna rose from her seat to greet her. She was dressed in a slinky black bandage halter top and shorts. She was barefoot. The AK-47 was nowhere in sight.

"You must feel naked without your rifle," Kate said.

"You're right," Reyna said. "I do."

"I'm sure you have other weapons."

"All women do," she said with a smile.

Kate wasn't sure if Reyna wanted to seduce her or kill her. Maybe it was both.

"Help yourself to the seafood. It was all caught fresh today. Mr. Violante doesn't like eating anything that has been dead for more than a few hours. The oysters are particularly good."

And supposedly they were an aphrodisiac, though definitely not for Kate. They looked like snot in a shell to her. Oreos were her idea of a culinary turn-on. And a Toblerone bar gave her ideas.

Kate picked up a plate and took a few shrimp and some crab legs while Reyna poured them both sangrias from a large pitcher filled with sliced fruit.

"How did you and Mr. Violante hook up?" Kate asked, taking a seat.

"He wanted the best security in Marbella. That was me. Pretty straightforward." Reyna swallowed an oyster and tossed the shell onto the table.

"Where did you get your training?" Kate broke open a crab leg and sucked out the meat.

"That's classified," Reyna said, and ate another oyster. "Where did you get yours?"

"University of Washington, followed by a few years at the Scripps Institution of Oceanography in San Diego."

"I meant military," Reyna said.

"I've never served."

"You're comfortable around weapons. You weren't afraid of the AK-47."

"That's because it wasn't pointed at me."

Kate had been counting down the minutes. She had a small window of opportunity to bug the house communications system, and that window was about to open. She grimaced and clutched her stomach. "Uh-oh."

Reyna raised an eyebrow. "What's wrong?"

"I think the crab is fighting back, or maybe I ate some bad cheese this afternoon. Where's the bathroom?"

"Behind you and to the left."

Kate already knew that. She'd seen it the first time she was here, and she'd spotted the bathroom window on her reconnaissance run earlier that day.

She hurried to the bathroom, closed the door, and locked it behind her. The bathroom was huge, with two sinks and enough marble for a family mausoleum. She figured that she had five minutes, tops, before Reyna came to check on her.

Kate opened the window, hiked herself up into it, and climbed out. She wasn't worried about being seen by security cameras. They were all aimed to watch for intruders on the grounds and along the perimeter. She checked her watch one last time.

There was a wrought-iron balcony outside the study and the bathroom, and an awning over the French doors that opened to the study. She climbed onto the railing, grasped the awning's wrought-iron supports, and hoisted herself onto the awning, careful to put her weight on the support struts and not the fabric. She crawled onto the roof and went straight to the satellite dish. Crouching down, she slipped off her right shoe and slid the sole off, revealing a hidden compartment. She removed the thin thumb-drive-size bugging device that she'd picked up in Lisbon.

She clipped the device to the cable that ran from the satellite dish to the house. The device was designed to bug the data stream and send a copy to the FBI using the same satellite that it was all flowing through. It was simple and ingenious. Jessup would be able to take down Violante and his whole organization with the information obtained from the bug.

Kate slid down the awning, slipped back into the bathroom, and closed the window behind her. She splashed water on her face and flushed the toilet. She left the bathroom and returned to Reyna.

"I'm going to skip dinner and go to bed," Kate said. "I'd avoid the crab if I were you."

Back at the guesthouse, Kate found a large platter of golden chocolates on the kitchen table. She doubted it was delivered as a gesture of hospitality. More likely, it was a pretense so the guards could nose around and see what she'd been up to all day. Or maybe it was like a maid checking the hotel minibar. Maybe they were keeping track of what she'd eaten so they could deduct the cost from the $17.5 million.

She settled herself onto the couch and switched on the television. She surfed around, looking for a show she wanted to watch, and fell asleep before she found one. When she awoke, the television was off and her father was standing at the kitchen table.

"We're going to have to work on your unconscious alarm system," he said. "I've been here moving around for five minutes, and you've only now opened your eyes."

He was dressed in black and was studying the platter of chocolates.

"I don't see much difference between these and a Hershey's Kiss except that you can eat the wrapper on these," he said.

"What the heck are you doing here?"

"You told me to have fun," Jake said. "This is fun."

"How did you get past the cameras and the guards?"

"I came in through Violante's secret escape tunnel. I found the hidden exit at the bottom of the gorge. It wasn't hard to spot if you know what you're looking for. The other end is right here in the coat closet." Jake gestured to a closet beside the front door. "The whole closet is actually a small elevator. You turn a particular coat hook counterclockwise and off you go."

"They're holding me hostage in the same room as their secret escape route?" Kate shook her head. "How dumb is that?"

"You didn't know it was here, did you?" Jake said, taking a bite of chocolate.

"No," she said.

"There you go. That's why they call it a *secret* escape route."

She was glad to see Jake, but having him here complicated things for her, and it left Nick and the crew vulnerable.

"What about the boat?" she asked. "Without you, there's nobody in charge or watching out for the crew. And what about Willie? She can't handle the boat on her own. She doesn't know what she's doing."

"Relax. They are all in good hands. Billy Dee has hijacked plenty of boats, most of them a lot bigger than this one, and steered them through the Gulf of Aden and the Red Sea with just two men. So this is a pleasure cruise for him. And Nick is on top of everything else."

"Does he know you're here?"

"Nick didn't send me," Jake said. "But he was glad when I told him where I was going."

"He wasn't concerned that you were putting the entire operation at risk?"

"He cares more about you than any operation."

"Only because I keep him from being arrested." She saw her father sway and grab the table for support. "Dad? What's wrong?"

"Feeling sleepy . . . too sleepy. Gotta be the chocolates."

Kate rushed forward, catching her father before he hit the floor. She took his pulse and noted his color. He was out cold, but he wasn't critical. His vital signs were all strong. She looked over at the candy display.

Reyna had drugged the chocolate.

At least she was fairly certain the candy wasn't laced with

lethal poison, and that her father would eventually be fine. There was no upside for Violante or Reyna in killing her. At least not yet.

So why did Reyna need her helpless and compliant? There were only a few possible answers, and none of them were pleasant. The one thing Kate was sure of was that Reyna would be paying her a visit tonight.

Kate dragged Jake into the bedroom and stretched him out beside the bed, out of sight from the door. She turned the lights off in all the rooms and waited in the darkness for Reyna.

Reyna arrived about an hour later. Kate could see her outside, through the edge of the closed drapes, propping her AK-47 outside the door. Kate assumed the rifle was a sign for the guards, letting them know where she was. Reyna adjusted the large satchel that she had over her shoulder, slipped inside the house, and crept toward the bedroom with remarkable stealth.

Kate flattened herself against a wall in the bedroom, and when Reyna entered the room, Kate whacked her in the head with a frying pan she'd commandeered from the kitchen. Reyna went dead still for a moment, then crumpled to the floor with a hiss of air.

Kate flipped the light on, lifted the satchel off Reyna's shoulder, and emptied it out onto the bed. It contained four nylon cords, rubber gloves, a pair of needle-nose pliers, and a filet knife. She looked back down at Reyna. "I don't even want to think about what you were going to do with this."

...

Jake started coming around as the tiny, rickety elevator dropped down the narrow shaft. He was on the floor, his back against one of the three elevator walls. Kate stood across from him, watching the sharp, rocky face of the shaft passing by on the open side where the closet door had been. The only light in the pitch-dark shaft came from the flashlight app on her father's cellphone.

"Take it easy, Dad," Kate said. "We're in the elevator."

"What happened after I passed out?"

"Reyna paid me a visit with pliers, a filet knife, and some nylon cords."

"She was going to tie you up, pull out some fingernails or teeth, and maybe peel off a few layers of skin," he said. "That wasn't very friendly."

"I'll say."

"Did you strangle her with your underwire?"

"Nope," Kate said. "The garrote is in my other bra."

"Another missed opportunity," Jake said. "Is she alive?"

"Of course she is. Killing her would have messed up the whole con. But she'll be tied up for a while. I bound her arms and legs to the bedposts with the nylon cords and gagged her with a towel. She'd left her AK-47 outside the guest house, warning off the guards, so we have some time before she either escapes from the ropes or is discovered."

They hit bottom, and Jake got shakily to his feet. "There's a deer trail through the gorge," he said. "I left a Jeep on a fire road about two miles south of here."

"Are you up for a walk?"

"Sure am," Jake said. "I had a nice, restful nap."

"What's the plan after we get to the car?"

"We've got rooms at the Marbella Club."

It was a five-star hotel, the posh resort of royals and movie stars. It had put Marbella on the map back in the 1950s, and it hadn't lost any of its cachet since then.

"Nick has been a bad influence on you," Kate said.

"Nick made the reservations for us. He said it was the FBI's treat to thank us for our trouble."

22

Nick knocked on Violante's door and took him up to the deck shortly after daybreak. The skies were clear and there was nothing but wide-open sea in all directions. They could have been anywhere on earth.

Billy Dee operated the crane, lifting up the ROV and lowering it down to the water on the starboard side of the boat. Violante stood at the starboard railing, intently watching the process.

Nick handed Violante a cup of coffee. "It will be a half hour before it reaches the bottom," Nick said. "Then the fun begins."

They stood at the rail and watched the ROV sink below the surface, slowly disappearing into the murk, until all they could see was the tether line and umbilical cable that the ROV was dragging down with it.

Rodney Smoot was sequestered in the cargo hold, ready to

put his render farm to work. "We're all set down here whenever you are," Rodney said into Nick's earbud. "We can pick up the video feed on descent if you want to get an early start on the show."

"We could watch the feed on descent, but it's pretty boring stuff," Nick said to Violante. "I suggest we grab some breakfast and then make our way to the command center."

The message was said to Violante, but meant for Rodney.

"Gotcha," Rodney said. "The opening credits and theme song are all cued up."

"Are we on top of the shipwreck?" Violante asked, following Nick to the deckhouse.

"More or less," Nick replied. "We'll have to do some traveling underwater to get there."

Violante followed Nick to the galley and helped himself to bread and ham and fresh figs. He topped off his coffee, and stood. He was ready to get on with his adventure. Nick took the hint and walked Violante down the corridor to the command center.

Violante paused for a moment in the doorway, letting his eyes adjust to the darkness. He stared at the array of buttons, monitors, keyboards, and joysticks. It wasn't necessary to know what any of it did. It was a big, shiny thing, and he was drawn to it like a salmon to a fishing lure.

"This is the heart and soul of our operation, the driver's seat of the ROV," Nick said to Violante.

Tom Underhill had been at the controls, but he gave up his

chair to Nick when Nick came into the room. Nick took the seat and steered the ROV slowly over the seabed.

In the silence and darkness of the command center, Violante's eyes fixed on the screen, and he felt as if he were swimming in the depths toward the treasure himself. His throat was dry and his heart was pounding. He hadn't been this anxious or excited in years. The anticipation was almost unbearable and yet wonderful at the same time.

"Would it be possible for me to take a turn at the joystick?" Violante asked.

"Sure," Nick said, vacating the seat. "Just think of this as a videogame. There's a large outcropping of jagged rock coming up. You want to make sure you steer around it."

Violante wrapped his hand around the stick and cautiously moved the ROV. The outcropping of rock appeared on the screen and Violante veered off to one side to avoid it. When the ROV cleared the rock Violante caught sight of the golden table, sticking upright out of the muck ahead, gleaming in the light cast by the ROV. The picture Hartley had shown him in Marbella hadn't fully captured the grandeur of the riches in the murk of the ocean floor. The radiance of the gold on the table, and the intricate engravings on the legs, showed through the concretions that stuck to the table like dollops of brown plaster.

Violante was so caught up in what he was seeing that he stopped paying attention to his driving, and the screen shuddered as the ROV scraped the side of a large rock.

"You break it, you buy it," Hartley said. "You've scraped the entire left side of the ROV against that rock. Looks like you took a light off."

"Sorry about that," Violante said, allowing the ROV to hover in place. "But it hardly matters in comparison to this vast wealth."

It mattered to Tom, who heard Nick's helpfully precise description of the damage through their earbud communications system. Tom signaled to Billy Dee in the crane to bring up the ROV. They'd have to replicate the damage to the vehicle before Violante showed up on deck. And they had to do it without damaging the vehicle so much that they revealed it was a hollow fake inside. It pained him to have to take a claw hammer to his beautiful creation.

The only thing that could have made the vision in front of Violante more dreamlike for him was if a mermaid swam by, beckoning him with her smile.

Beyond the splendid table, as far as the scope of the lights could reach in the murk, were piles of coins that had once been stored in wooden crates. The crates had long since rotted away, spilling the coins onto the ocean floor. Golden plates, goblets, flatware, candlesticks, and trinket boxes were scattered along with the coins, concretion-covered cannons, and cannonballs. It was a field of splendor, wealth, and legend beyond Violante's wildest imagination. It was a boyhood fantasy come true.

He looked past the gold and noticed something that didn't

fit. There were black boxes, the size of bricks, with tiny antennas on them. The boxes were spread in strategic spots around the table and the piles of coins and they were connected to one another with a blue cable.

"What are those boxes?" Violante asked.

"Insurance policies," Hartley said. "Explosive charges capable of reducing all of this gold to dust and scattering it over a wide area, perhaps miles with the current."

It sickened Violante that Hartley could even think about destroying something so glorious, so rare. Blowing up price-less riches that have withstood centuries in the deep would be a terrible crime, certainly worse than anything he had ever done. People could be replaced. But good luck finding a one-ton solid gold table anywhere.

"Destroying those priceless, irreplaceable artifacts would be sacrilege," Violante said. "Unforgivable."

"As an archaeologist by training, I agree with you," Hartley said. "So don't make me do it. If you want this, pay me for it."

"You don't have a very high opinion of me."

"Just being careful," Hartley said. "Would you like to take some souvenirs home with you?"

"Absolutely."

"Pick a pile of coins, and we'll scoop some of them up," Nick said.

Violante pointed to the pile directly in front of them. "Those will do."

Nick showed Violante how to use the left robotic arm to

remove a white plastic bucket from the ROV and hold it steady on the seabed while using the right robotic arm to shovel coins into it. The process took about forty-five minutes, and Violante enjoyed every second of it.

The experience brought back a childhood memory. He was at an arcade with his dad and tried one of those coin-operated machines that gave you a chance to scoop up a stuffed rabbit with a joystick-operated claw hand. He wasn't able to get the animal and threw a fit. His father smashed the glass and gave him the stuffed animal. When the manager came over and chastised them, his father shot the man in the face. It was a happy moment. This would be too. Maybe he'd shoot Nick Hartley in the face to come full circle.

Violante used the right arm to put a lid on the bucket, and used the left arm to secure the bucket to the ROV.

"Excellent," Nick said. "You've really got the hang of it. Time to bring the ROV back up to the surface. I'll take over the controls now."

Violante stood behind Nick and watched the ROV trace its path back around the outcropping of rock, skim over the ocean floor, and make a slow ascent. The screen went black and Violante gasped.

"What happened?" he asked.

"The crane operator has taken over," Nick said. "Our ROV is being lifted out of the water. Time for us to go on deck."

Nick and Violante reached the starboard railing just as the ROV was carefully set on the deck. The left side of the ROV was badly scraped, chrome hanging from the nacelle and a large gash where one of the side lights had been. Nick thought Tom had done a great job replicating the damage Violante had supposedly caused.

There was a white bucket on a shelf underneath the nose of the craft. Tom stepped up, lifted the wet, heavy bucket out of the ROV, brought it over to Nick and Violante, and set it down at their feet.

Nick handed Violante a pair of rubber gloves. "Put these on. The concretions on the gold can be sharp."

Tom lifted the lid off the bucket, which was filled with murky water and smelled like rotting fish. Violante reached into the cold water and came out with a handful of coins. The coins were dripping with muck, but the gold still shone through, glittering in the sunlight.

"Magnificent," he said, and dropped the coins back into the bucket.

"It's time for you to go back to your room," Nick said. "Take the bucket with you, if you like."

Violante replaced the lid and carried the bucket back to the deckhouse. He stopped at the door to his cabin and turned to Nick.

"I want the treasure," Violante said.

"I want eighteen million dollars," Nick said.

"You mean seventeen and a half million dollars."

"That was before you damaged my ROV," Nick said.

Violante grimaced as if feeling physical pain, and Nick knew that Violante was checking his temper, resisting the urge to strangle him on the spot.

"I'll want maps, sonar readings, anything and everything I will need to precisely locate the wreck," Violante said. "And I will need those bombs removed."

"Of course. All part of our customer service. I will need the money in cash."

"Do you realize how much cash that is?"

"Enough to fill a bathtub, and that's just what I might do with it."

"It's going to be extremely difficult to gather that much cash quickly and without attracting unwanted attention."

"That's *your* problem."

"Be reasonable. It would be so much easier, and more discreet, for me to draw the funds from various accounts around the globe and put them directly into your preferred bank account."

"I want cash," Nick said. "It's a deal breaker for me."

Violante narrowed his eyes as best he could, considering his face was stretched as tight as a drum. "Why?"

"The same reason you wanted to stick your hands into the bucket and hold the coins in your fingers. I want something I can hold in my hands, or bathe in, or scatter around my bedroom. I'm not getting the coins, or the shiny gold table, so this is as close as I am going to get to tangible treasure. I need to be able to look at it, to feel it, to admire it. I know you understand."

Violante nodded. "I'll see what I can do."

"I'll call you a day before I want to meet and give you the details of the transaction."

Nick locked Violante into his cabin with his gold, and went up to the bridge. Willie was at the helm and Boyd was slumped in the captain's chair, watching the activity on deck, and looking generally mopey.

"Congratulations, Nick," Willie said. "That was a great show."

"Thank you. We'll head back to Málaga tonight," Nick said. "Is something wrong, Boyd?"

"I was expecting a larger role in the action. Instead, I've been stuck up here with Willie."

"At least you could leave," Willie said. "I can't. I have to drive the boat. I've been a captive audience. Do you think it's a joy having to listen to you blather on all day about your fictional life at sea while you hobble around the bridge, bumping into things?"

"I've made an effort to stay in character, to add depth and color to my performance, not that it was put to much use."

"It's true you had a supporting part, and not the lead, but you were perfect," Nick said. "You exuded authority and were the key player in establishing the realism of our charade. Violante was utterly convinced by your character. Besides, you still have another role to play before this con is over."

"Is it a juicy part?"

"It's pivotal."

Nick's cellphone rang, and he knew from the ringtone that it was Jake calling. He was surprised when he heard Kate's voice at the other end.

"I'm poolside at the Marbella Club drinking sangrias and working on my tan," Kate said.

"Nice. I'm assuming the hostage thing didn't work out for you."

"Reyna's hostess skills leave a lot to be desired. Dad showed up at just the right time last night and took a chocolate for me."

"Don't you mean a bullet?"

"Reyna laced the chocolates in my room with knockout drops and Dad ate one. I returned the favor and left Reyna tied to the bedposts. I loaded Dad into the secret elevator, and here we are, leading the good life."

"What was your weapon of choice?"

"Frying pan."

"Nice to know you have a domestic side," Nick said. "Did Reyna see your father?"

"Nope," Kate said. "She was unconscious when we left, and I sent the elevator back up to the closet so it wouldn't be immediately obvious how I escaped."

"Then we're fine," he said. "We'll express our anger at your treatment by jacking up the price by two million dollars."

"Violante isn't going to be happy about any of this," Kate said.

"No, but he has no leverage. We have the gold. He's seen it, and now he wants it. So he'll apologize, pay the extra money with a smile, and plan on getting his retribution later."

23

It was midafternoon before one of Violante's guards began to wonder exactly what was going on in the guesthouse and was brave enough to ignore the AK-47 by the front door. He found Reyna Socorro tied up spread-eagle on the king-size bed with a gag in her mouth. He untied her, and as soon as circulation returned to her hands, she broke his neck.

As much as she appreciated being found after sixteen hours, she couldn't let anyone live who'd seen her subjugated and powerless. If she had, she would certainly have lost whatever authority she had over her men. He had to die, but she knew it wasn't fair and offered her sincere apology to his corpse.

She inspected the guesthouse for possible avenues of escape and finally reached the conclusion that Kate had gone out the front door and somehow eluded the guard. He'd probably been asleep on the job and deserved to die, Reyna thought. She assembled her security force and told them to search the compound. She returned to the guesthouse and reconsidered the closet. If somehow Kate had discovered the secret elevator, she was long gone. Probably in London by now. The elevator simply looked like a closet. Hard to believe Kate was resourceful enough to realize that the closet was an elevator and rotate the coat hook.

Reyna reached for a chocolate and instantly snatched her hand back. She'd already lost half a day. She didn't need to drug herself and lose more time. The Hartley bitch was most likely hiding on the property somewhere, and when she was found she'd pay dearly.

Reyna's equipment was still spread out on the bed, including the throwaway cellphone that connected her to Nick Hartley. A feeling of dread swept over her when the phone rang. She thought Nick was most likely calling in a ransom demand, and she'd lost her hostage. Not good. She was beginning to wonder if perhaps the smartest thing she could do, for her own survival, was to take whatever cash she could from the house, make a run for it now, and hope that she could hide from Violante, if he lived, or from the Menendez cartel, if he didn't.

She took a beat to compose herself and answered the call.

"We're going to be returning to port around eight A.M. tomorrow morning," Hartley said, his tone upbeat and jovial. "I suggest that you and Kate get there early, just so Mr. Violante isn't kept waiting if we arrive ahead of schedule, but that's entirely up to you. It's a suggestion, not a demand."

Reyna was confused. Hartley wasn't asking for ransom, and he didn't seem to know that his wife had escaped.

"We'll be there," Reyna said.

"Can I speak to Kate?"

"I don't know where she is right now," Reyna said. "It's a big property, and she has the run of it."

"No problem," Hartley said. "I'll see you both tomorrow morning."

Reyna disconnected and flipped the phone back onto the bed. When her men finished searching the compound she'd send them to search the brush at the bottom of the gorge. With any luck the Hartley woman was down on the rocks with her head burst open like a water balloon.

Two black Range Rovers, the Mercedes, and Violante's security team were already on the dock when the ship arrived. Violante lugged his bucket of gold coins and salt water down the gangway to meet Reyna, who was waiting for them at the bottom.

Violante could tell right away that something was wrong. Reyna had her AK-47 slung over her shoulder, the guards were tense, and Kate Hartley was nowhere to be seen.

He could only draw one horrible conclusion. Reyna had ignored his orders and tortured Kate, probably to death.

Reyna met his icy gaze. "How was your trip?"

"Excellent," Violante said. "I saw the wreck and brought back some coins. Nick will be calling us with payment details."

"I'm glad to hear that," Reyna said. "We'll do whatever we can to make the transaction as smooth as possible."

"Where's my wife?" Hartley asked.

"Good question," Reyna said. "She seems to have vanished."

Hartley glanced back at the ship where the captain and three other members of the crew were on deck, shouldering rifles.

"Vanished?" Nick asked. "Do you want to clarify that?"

A taxi drove down the wharf and came to a stop behind the Mercedes. Kate got out of the taxi, carrying shopping bags from Escada and Gucci.

"Reyna told us you vanished," Nick said to his wife.

"I did," Kate said, setting her bags on the pavement. "I vanished after Reyna sneaked into my room with her torture kit. Fortunately, I was in the kitchen and not in bed as she expected." Kate smiled, obviously pleased with herself. "I hit her with a frying pan!"

"Good for you," Nick said, equally pleased. "Now if you could just learn how to cook with one."

"I wish you'd get on with it," Rodney Smoot said into Nick's earbud. "This rifle's getting heavy."

Nick turned his attention back to Violante.

"Before you do anything else stupid," Nick said to Violante, "let me remind you that the shipwreck is rigged with explosives and if anything happens to me or my wife, my crew will destroy the treasure. All the captain has to do is press a button."

"Nothing is going to happen," Violante said. "Everybody stay calm. We can work this out amicably."

"She had a filet knife and pliers!" Kate said.

"Reyna is very loyal to me," Violante said. "I rescued her from a culture where violence is a way of life. It's all she knows, and I have been trying to change that. But she was convinced that I was being tricked, that you were kidnapping me, and she expressed her admirable concern for my life. She only wanted to be sure that I was safe."

"Twenty-five million," Kate said. "That's the new price. I'm going to need therapy after this experience."

It was an outrageous demand, but Violante was relieved to hear it. It meant the deal wasn't dead. And it also meant he'd been right that their greed trumped everything. She wanted his money as much as he wanted their gold.

"Twenty-five in cash. It's nonnegotiable," Kate said. "Take it or leave it."

Nick nodded his agreement. "Twenty-five in cash."

"Done," Violante said without hesitation.

"You have three days to get the cash together," Nick said. "We'll be in touch."

"You violated my orders and nearly jeopardized everything," Violante said to Reyna as they sat side by side in the backseat of the car on their way to Marbella. "Give me one good reason why I shouldn't kill you."

"I'm the one who does your killing."

"I can get someone else to kill you. There are lots of people who would *love* to kill you. I wouldn't even have to pay them."

"The Hartleys aren't what they seem."

"Neither are we. What matters is that they came offering to sell the location of a magnificent treasure. I've seen the treasure and I've got a bucket of it. So as far as I'm concerned, they are playing straight with me, whoever they are," Violante said. "The only reason you're still alive is because we haven't lost the deal."

And because he had no one he trusted to take her place.

"That was fun, making them sweat," Kate said to Nick as they reached the ship's deck.

"And we got to stick them for a few million dollars more, which is something I always like to do." He looked at the bags Kate was carrying. "Looks like you're already spending our money."

"I didn't have any fancy-hotel-worthy clothes," Kate said. "I left the tags on and kept the receipts so I can return everything when we get to Lisbon."

"We're not going back to Lisbon. We'd be under constant surveillance there by Alves or Violante's people from the moment we docked. You're leaving us here and flying to London while the rest of us go to Tangier and split up there."

"Makes sense," Kate said. "What happens to the ship?"

"Billy Dee will sell it for us in return for a generous commission. The ship will be renamed, reflagged, and back out to sea in a couple weeks."

"And what happens to the money you get from selling the boat?"

"It goes back into our slush fund for illegal derring-do," Nick said. "Where's Jake?"

Kate gestured to the dock. "Dad was covering us from beside one of the warehouses on the waterfront."

Nick looked toward the warehouses and saw Jake walking toward the ship, a rocket-propelled grenade launcher slung over his shoulder.

"When did he pick *that* up?" Nick asked.

"Before he came to visit me in Marbella. He knows arms dealers everywhere and doesn't feel secure without a few explosives handy. If things had gone south here today, he would have blown up the two Range Rovers, and I would have opened up with the Uzi I'm carrying in my Gucci bag."

"It's so important to accessorize correctly," Nick said.

24

Kate called Jessup as soon as she got to London and settled into her small room at the Radisson Sussex.

"The intel has already started streaming in from Menendez's computer," Jessup said. "He's gathering the cash to pay Nick and, in the process, he's leading us to all his offshore accounts. We're talking hundreds of millions of dollars. But that's not the best part. We're getting a real-time overview of his entire global operation and international smuggling routes."

"You can't act on any of that until we have him in custody or you'll spook him. I'd like you to call Scotland Yard. Tell them I've just arrived in heated pursuit of two international fugitives and that the FBI requests their immediate tactical assistance to arrest them and prevent a major crime from occurring in London."

"So much for staying below the radar," Jessup said. "Are you actually arresting any fugitives in London?"

"We're going to try. We're setting up the money drop here."

A couple hours after the call, Kate walked a half block to the food court at Selfridges department store. It was her favorite place to eat in London. Kate ordered a chicken and mushroom pie, a steak and cheese pie, and a side of mushy peas, a British dish made of marrowfat and peas soaked in baking soda and simmered in water, sugar, and salt to form a delicious lumpy green glop. She got a Coke to wash it all down and carried her tray to a table in the large communal dining hall.

She devoured the chicken pie and half of her mushy peas and was about to take on her steak pie when a middle-aged man sat down at her table. He had a cup of tea and three glazed Krispy Kreme donuts stacked like poker chips on a napkin. His disheveled hair was flecked with gray, his eyes were bloodshot, and his ruddy cheeks were covered with stubble. He wore a long, beat-up leather coat with wide sheepskin-lined lapels that were almost as brown as the cracked and faded hide. The coat was open showing a white Oxford shirt and a loosely knotted red-and-yellow-striped polyester tie. He was her kind of cop.

"Do you live in that coat?" Kate asked.

"Pretty much," he replied in an accent that betrayed his Manchester roots. "It goes with everything. If I ever get married, I'll wear it down the aisle."

Kate grinned at the thought and offered her hand. "FBI Special Agent Kate O'Hare."

"DCI Dennis Gooley. How did you make me as a copper?"

She pointed with her fork to the donuts. "Dead giveaway."

"And my strong moral posture."

"That, too," she said. "How did you find me?"

"I run the Flying Squad, that's our specialist crime and operations section, and this is my patch. You can't take a leak in the street without me knowing about it." He took a sip of his tea. "So why do you need our assistance?"

"Nicolas Fox is meeting Lester Menendez here in forty-eight hours. I want to nail them both."

He took another sip of tea. "Maybe after that we can capture the Loch Ness monster and D. B. Cooper, too."

"I'm not joking."

"You're telling me that two of the most-wanted fugitives on the planet are going to be together in London?"

"I am. And in the same room."

Gooley shook his head, skeptical. "If you say Fox will be here, I can believe that. But nobody knows who Menendez is now or what he looks like."

"He'll be the guy meeting with Nicolas Fox."

Gooley smiled. "Cute."

"I come by it naturally."

"Tell me how you got onto Menendez. The way I heard it, you were chasing Fox for a string of museum heists. But it wasn't him, it was his protégé Serena Blake masquerading as Fox to throw the coppers off her scent."

"I thought so," she said. "But I was wrong."

"But you caught her in the act."

"That's exactly what it was." Kate started working on her steak pie while he ate his second donut. "Serena was partnering with Fox all along. That's why she wouldn't cut a deal in return for telling us where she'd stashed the stuff that she stole. Because Fox has it all."

"I don't get it. Why would Fox want Serena Blake to go running around the world stealing things and framing him for the heists?"

"She was a diversion. Fox was using her to drag us around the globe while he was here in London, planning his next big heist and selling the stolen art to finance the job."

"What's he going after?"

"The crown jewels."

Gooley looked at Kate like she'd grown two heads. "That's insane. The closest anyone has come to stealing the crown jewels was in 1671, and it failed. And back then it was easy. All you had to do was hit a dumb bloke over the head with a mallet. Security is a bit tighter now."

"The impossibility of stealing the crown jewels is what makes it irresistible to Fox. He's been planning the robbery for years, and my intel says he's ready to do it."

"Where does Menendez fit into this?"

"He doesn't know it, but he's helping to finance the robbery,"

Kate said. "He's paying twenty-five million dollars for the stuff that Serena Blake stole."

"That's a hell of a story," Gooley said, grabbing a paper napkin and wiping the sugar off his fingers. "How did you find out all of that?"

Kate pushed her plate aside. She was about to tell a lot of lies mixed with just enough half truths to make her story convincing. At least, that was her hope.

"Are you familiar with Duff MacTaggert?" she asked Gooley.

"I've spent most of my career trying to put him away and never even got close, though we did have fish and chips once," Gooley said. "Ran into each other at the same greasy takeaway in Soho. It was like that scene between Pacino and De Niro in *Heat,* except we had nothing to say to each other, so we just stood there talking about football and the weather, and that was that. I hear the bastard has retired to some tropical island in Indonesia where the law can't touch him."

"It's called Dajmaboutu. I've got a source, one of the Torajan natives on MacTaggert's household staff. She told me that MacTaggert set up a meeting between Fox and Diogo Alves, a black market middleman in Lisbon. I arrived in Portugal too late to catch them together, but I followed Alves to Demetrio Violante, a wealthy and mysterious developer in Marbella. He's practically a recluse, and nobody knows anything about him. A few months after Menendez vanished, Violante suddenly appeared in Marbella and brutally muscled his way to the top of the construction business."

"That doesn't make him Menendez."

"Violante has the same bone structure as Menendez, he's got no past, and his head of security is Reyna Socorro, an ex–Colombian rebel who joined the Menendez cartel shortly before Menendez disappeared."

"It's still circumstantial."

"Don't you ever have a gut feeling that you can't ignore?" Kate asked.

"The way I eat, yeah. Almost every day."

"You know what I mean. Do you trust your instincts?"

"It's not a question of whether I trust mine," Gooley said. "It's whether I can trust yours."

"Violante is coming here Thursday with twenty-five million in cash to buy a Matisse, a Vermeer, and a jewel-encrusted sultan's goblet. Worst-case scenario, Violante is not Menendez, and we arrest Fox on his dozens of international warrants. Plus you get to arrest some guy for buying millions of dollars' worth of stolen art and antiquities. As an added bonus, we prevent the heist of the crown jewels. Unless, of course, you have something better to do."

"Nothing that can't wait. Do you know where this meeting is going down?"

"The Excelsior Tower, eighteenth floor."

"Perfect. I can put you up in shouting distance, so you can keep it under surveillance. Get your bags, check out of the hotel, and let's go take a look-see."

...

The Excelsior Tower was twenty stories of pitch-darkness, even darker than the night sky. It was as if a black hole had opened up on the south bank of the Thames, right in the middle of the five-hundred-yard stretch of river that ran between the Albert Bridge to the east and the Battersea Bridge to the west.

Kate and Gooley leaned against Gooley's illegally parked Vauxhall Insignia and studied the Excelsior from the Chelsea Embankment. The monolith of glass and marble was curved to embrace a pool, tennis courts, and a private marina where several yachts were docked.

"Why is the building so dark?" Kate asked. "Is it unoccupied?"

Gooley lit a cigarette. "There are eighty flats in there. The least expensive is twenty million pounds. The penthouses are over a hundred million. Sixty-nine of the flats have been sold. Mostly to dictators, warlords, mobsters, and Russian oligarchs." Gooley blew a stream of smoke out toward the river. "Lovely blokes who don't want you to know who they are or how they got their dirty money."

"Nicolas Fox's kind of people," Kate said. "Who owns the other apartments?"

"A Ukrainian mining magnate, a Taiwanese drug company giant, a Nigerian telecommunications billionaire, a couple of sheiks, and I don't know who else. The Malcolms, the British couple that developed the property, are the only ones who actually live in the building. The others visit maybe for a week or two each year."

"I imagine security is very tight."

"Armed guards, private elevators, retina scanners, fingerprint access pads, the works."

"And the perks?"

"A concierge staff that will do your grocery shopping for you. Also saunas, a movie theater, and a virtual golf course with a full-time flesh-and-blood golf pro."

"My building has a coin-operated washer and dryer," Kate said.

"Mine doesn't even have that," Gooley said.

"Security, exclusivity, and outrageous luxury," Kate said. "I can see why Fox picked the Excelsior. He's going to feel very comfortable there."

"We'll have eyes, including yours, on that building 24/7 within the hour."

"He's got a sixth sense about surveillance," Kate said. "He won't be fooled by fake utility workers and female cops pushing baby carriages."

"That's not a problem. The entire city is covered with CCTV cameras. The only place we don't have them yet is up your bum." Gooley turned and pointed to a grand old apartment house that faced the Excelsior. "We'll also set up a dedicated camera and a laser microphone in that building and aim them both at his flat. We'll see and hear everything."

"Unless he closes the blinds," Kate said. "Then we won't see a thing."

"He won't close them. You don't buy a place like that and bring somebody over to see it unless you want to impress them with the view and show them that you're king of the city." Gooley tossed his cigarette butt onto the street and stubbed it out under his shoe. "I'm sure you want to plant yourself someplace where you can keep your eye on the building without being seen, so I've got a nice surprise for you."

Gooley popped the trunk, grabbed Kate's duffel bag, and led her down to Cadogan Pier. It was underneath the first span of the Albert Bridge and ran parallel to the Chelsea Embankment. A dozen barge-like houseboats, a couple sporty yachts, and some small pleasure craft were moored there.

Gooley stopped in front of a sixty-five-foot yacht that looked like a smaller version of the one Nick had borrowed in Marina del Rey. A small motorized dinghy was tied to the yacht's swim deck.

"We seized this yacht a month ago from a villain in the white slavery trade," Gooley said. "It's due to go up for auction, but in the meantime it's just bobbing around here. So far as I know it's just as it was when we took possession with bed linens and such. I figure you might as well use it. As I remember there's even a pair of binoculars inside, unless someone's snitched them. I'll pick you up tomorrow, bring you back to the Yard, and we'll go over the details of the operation. The key is under the doormat."

The yacht was furnished like a five-star hotel, with lots of marble, leather, and polished wood. The binoculars were on the dinette table. Kate picked them up and looked at the eighteenth-floor river-facing suite where the exchange would go down. The lights were off and she couldn't see anything. Only one condo was lit in the building. It was on the ninth floor. Most likely the Malcolms'.

Nick called on her cellphone.

"I see you've settled in beside the Trembling Lady," Nick said.

"Is that the yacht parked beside mine?"

"It's what they call the Albert Bridge. It's been structurally unsound and shaking since the day it opened in 1874. There's still a sign on either end warning soldiers not to walk across it in step or the mechanical resonance could cause the bridge to collapse."

"Not much chance of any soldiers doing that today."

"What you've got to worry about is a dog relieving himself. Over a hundred and forty years of dog urine, from pooches being walked across the bridge to Battersea Park, have rotted the timber decks. This could be the day a pooch lifts his leg and takes the bridge down."

"You're making that up," she said. "Or it's an urban legend."

"It's the truth," Nick said. "I read it in a scholarly book on bridge engineering."

Kate shook her head in the dark privacy of the boat salon. Nick Fox was so full of baloney, and was such a convincing liar, that it was impossible to consistently separate fact from fiction. Even after working with him on several jobs she couldn't always tell when he was handing her a load of horse pucky.

"I've set up the meeting with Violante," Nick said. "We're good to go."

"It's going to be a major police operation. One tiny miscalculation and you'll end up in prison."

"Just another day at the office," he said.

She remembered her father saying the same thing over breakfast at Denny's a few weeks ago. The casual observation had been as true for Jake then as it was for Nick now. It wasn't the first time she'd been struck, and more than a little creeped out, by what the two most important men in her life had in common, besides her.

"Scotland Yard is running this," she said. "I won't be able to help you."

"What matters to me is that you wish you could," Nick said. "I think you're falling for me."

"That's a frightening thought," Kate said. "It sends chills down my spine."

It was a flip reply, but it had some truth to it. She lived in mortal fear of falling for him. What woman wouldn't fall for him? He was exciting and sexy and rich. He even smelled good. Appreciating his value as a partner was acceptable. Falling for him was terrifying.

25

Kate spent the next day at Scotland Yard planning the logistics of the stakeout and arrest with Gooley. He'd beefed up the plainclothes police presence in the Battersea Park area. The video feeds from the CCTV cameras were under constant observation. The dedicated surveillance camera and laser microphone were in place in the Chelsea apartment building, trained across the Thames at the Excelsior Tower's eighteenth floor.

Kate drank coffee and watched the live feed on monitors that were mounted on the wall of the squad room. The drapes of the Excelsior flat were closed, and no lights were on. Gooley assured Kate that if there was a fly in that room, they'd hear it buzzing. She'd been given a police radio, a Kevlar vest, and a yellow windbreaker with the word POLICE printed across the back, but it had been made clear that she was an observer and not a participant. Standard operating procedure, Kate thought. It was what it was.

At the end of the day, Gooley and two dozen of his detectives gathered in a conference room for one last briefing. The long table was covered with laptops, scattered papers, coffee cups, and takeout food containers. The walls were plastered with pictures of the Excelsior Tower, blueprints of the building, various photos of Nicolas Fox, and street maps.

Gooley took out a laser pointer and aimed the beam at the maps. "Let's go over it one more time. Fox is a pro. He's going to spot us on the street if we're watching, so we've got to hang back and rely on our cameras. We'll have our strike teams waiting in Battersea Park, and on the Chelsea side of the Battersea and Albert bridges, far enough away not to be noticed, but close enough to move in quickly when I give the word. And we'll also have a chopper in the air. Nobody moves in until I give the green light. At that point, we'll surround the building. We'll land blue team on the roof by chopper while red team secures the parking garage, yellow team secures the lobby, and green team seals the perimeter. The goal is complete containment."

Kate felt déjà vu throughout the briefing. She'd tried to spring a trap like this on Nick many times before and had given basically the same instructions to her teams. It took her quite a while, and several failures, to realize her mistake and think outside the box to capture him. Luckily for Nick, Gooley was still firmly inside the box.

"We can't assume the blueprints we have of the flats are

accurate," Gooley said. "There could be hidden safe rooms and escape routes that we don't know about. What we do know is that many of the flats have a private lift and, in some cases, a lift for the car as well. The good news is that it's a tower. There are basically only two ways out, from the top or from the bottom, and we'll have both ends covered. So once both men are inside that building, they are ours."

"But you can't move in until the exchange goes down," Kate said. "Or we've got nothing on Menendez."

"Exactly," Gooley said. "And we need to remember that whether it's Violante or Menendez, he's carrying the equivalent of twenty-five million dollars to this party. He's going to have a small army along with him for protection. We don't want this to become a firefight. But if it does, take them down hard and fast."

Kate and Gooley picked up fish and chips to go on the way back to the yacht. They ate the beer-battered cod and thick-cut fries outside on the flybridge with the Albert Bridge brightly lit behind them.

"Is it true that the Albert Bridge is rotted with dog pee?" Kate asked, dipping her fish in tartar sauce.

"Yeah, but they say they've fixed it. On the other hand, they've been fixing the bridge since the day it was opened, and it still shakes, so I don't buy it. This is a lousy stretch of the Thames for bridges." Gooley gestured to the Battersea Bridge behind her. Composed of five low cast-iron arches supported by granite pillars across a sharp bend in the Thames, it wasn't lit up in a showy fashion like the Albert. "That one is sturdier, but ships have been ramming into it for hundreds of years. A whale even got stuck underneath it a few years back. They've got the poor sod's skeleton in the natural history museum. I wouldn't want to be immortalized for the humiliating accident that killed me."

"How about as the guy who captured Nicolas Fox and Lester Menendez?"

"That'd be nice," Gooley said. "I could retire on that one."

"Aren't you too young to put in for your pension already?"

"Yeah, but I could live off the money from the hit movie based on the arrest," he said. "Russell Crowe can play me."

"He wouldn't wear that coat," Kate said. "And he's Australian."

"So what? Renée Zellweger wasn't British and she was Bridget Jones."

"Good point. Who is going to play me?"

"Renée Zellweger," Gooley said. "She could use her American accent this time."

Their radios crackled to life and a detective's voice came over the speaker. "The robin is in the nest."

Kate and Gooley turned in unison to look at the Excelsior Tower. Lights were on in the eighteenth-floor flat.

"Showtime," Gooley said, hauling a laptop out of a beat-up computer bag.

He set the laptop on the table, and pulled up the video feed from the Chelsea apartment building. The screen showed a large sparsely furnished space that looked more like an art gallery than a home. There were paintings on the walls and antiquities in display cases. The furniture was Swedish, contemporary, and looked as if it had been designed to stretch and dry hides. And standing in the middle of the room, stylishly dressed in a light-weight black sweater and black slacks, was Nicolas Fox. He was sipping from a mug, admiring a painting of a woman in a red dress.

"Can we zoom in tighter on him?" Gooley said into the radio.

The camera pushed in and it was clear that Nick was drinking from a golden jewel-encrusted goblet.

"The bugger is drinking from Suleiman the Magnificent's goblet," Gooley said. He squinted at the screen and tapped the painting with his finger. "Do you recognize that?"

Kate nodded. "It's the Vermeer that Serena Blake stole from Heiko Balz's bedroom while he was sleeping. Next to it is the Matisse from the Gleaberg Museum in Nashville. I'll bet the other paintings are stolen, too."

In fact, they were all pieces of art that Serena Blake had stolen over the years. This flat was her London pied-à-terre, compli-ments of a very wealthy, very old, very absent, very crooked German banker. On the three days out of the year that he used the flat he enjoyed looking at the art collection and didn't especially care how it happened to be on his walls.

Nick walked across the living room, and the camera panned to the kitchen, which had more stainless steel than a morgue.

He opened the refrigerator, took out a bottle of Coke, and refilled the goblet.

Kate knew that drinking Coke was something she'd do, not Nick. That was a hat tip to her.

"He's using the goblet to have a Coke? Bloody hell," Gooley said. "We ought to arrest him just for that."

"It's a goblet," Kate said. "They're made for drinking."

"If you're going to drink from a four-hundred-year-old goblet covered with jewels, it had better be the most expensive whisky that you can buy." He turned to Kate. "So what do you think? Should we take him down now? A bird in the hand?"

"Hell no. What kind of a movie would that make? I say we go for the big finale."

"Keep all eyes on the robin but do not approach," Gooley said into his radio. "Repeat. Do not approach."

"Russell Crowe will be pleased," Kate said.

26

Two silver Range Rovers crossed the Battersea Bridge from the Chelsea side of the Thames at 11 A.M. the next day.

Two armed men in business suits sat in the front seat of the lead Range Rover. The backseat was folded down to accommodate eight aluminum hard-shell suitcases, each containing the euro cash equivalent of slightly more than $3 million that had been withdrawn from a half dozen banks around London.

The second Range Rover carried two more armed men and, in the backseat, Demetrio Violante, who'd flown into London that morning. He wore a blue two-button Brioni wool and silk suit, an azure and blue micro-checked cotton shirt, a sky-blue silk tie, palladium cufflinks, and polished black calfskin derby dress shoes. He wasn't dressed for Hartley, for whom he had no respect. He was dressed for the money, which he respected enormously.

The cars drove to the south-facing entrance, which had the requisite grand portico adorned with polished marble and a large elaborate fountain.

Violante called Hartley on his cellphone.

"It's Demetrio Violante. I'm outside your building."

"Excellent. Come on up. Drive the car with the money into the garage. Do not bring anyone else with you. Park in lift number eighteen, roll down your driver's side window, and press the button on the wall. It will bring you up to my flat."

Violante didn't like it, not because he was concerned for his safety, but because he didn't want to unload the money from the car. Each suitcase weighed about seventy pounds. He'd had fat sucked out of every part of his body and the slack skin stitched tight. He didn't want to rupture something with physical exertion. Not to mention he was wearing a very nice suit.

"So you want me to drive the car into a lift in the garage and ride it up to your apartment," Violante said, getting out of his Range Rover and dismissing the guards in the other with a wave of his hand.

"Yes, that's right," Hartley said.

The guards got out of their car, and Violante climbed into the driver's seat. "How high up am I going?"

"The eighteenth floor."

"The eighteenth floor," Violante said.

"I hope you aren't afraid of heights."

No, he wasn't. He was repeating the instructions so Reyna, who was observing the exchange from a distance, would know exactly where he was and what he was doing. She was listening to everything through the flesh-colored radio device hidden deep in his other ear. He'd thought about holding the cellphone to that ear so she'd hear everything, but he was afraid that putting the two devices so close together might cause a shriek of feedback that would make him permanently deaf.

"We've got another pigeon in the coop," Gooley said over the radio.

Gooley was in Battersea Park, the staging area for the primary strike teams that were waiting to converge on the Excelsior Tower, a half block to the northwest. The other teams were waiting for the go-ahead on the Chelsea side of the Albert and Battersea bridges.

Kate didn't understand why Gooley didn't identity the suspects and locations by name. She practically needed a glossary to keep track of the code names for everything. Confusing officers about who was who, and what was what, was more dangerous than the possibility that bad guys might be listening in. Gooley's announcement that Violante had entered the Excelsior Tower had been redundant anyway. She'd heard Nick's instructions to Violante through her laptop, thanks to the laser mike pointed at his apartment from the building across the river.

She was in the yacht and was dressed for action in the Kevlar vest and bright yellow police windbreaker. She would have liked to accessorize the outfit with a Glock, but since she didn't have one with her, she settled for her collapsible baton.

The laptop was open in front of Kate, showing her a live close-up camera view of Nick's apartment. And if she lifted her head, she could look out her window at the Excelsior Tower directly across the river. It was like having a luxury suite at the Super Bowl. All that was missing was a buffet and a bartender.

She watched Nick bring out a bottle of champagne and an ice bucket and set it on a coffee table. He knew he was under visual and audio surveillance, that a ruthless killer was on the way up to his apartment, and that more than fifty heavily armed cops were close by, itching to arrest him. And yet he seemed completely at ease.

Kate was impressed by his control. Nobody was watching her, or coming to get her, but she could feel the mounting tension like a heat lamp over her head. Maybe he was just wired differently than the rest of humanity. Maybe *this* was how he relaxed, and being safe made him anxious.

If so, he was in for a very relaxing hour.

The lift moved with surprising speed and comfort, considering it was basically a freight elevator hauling a two-and-a-half-ton SUV up eighteen stories. When the lift reached the apartment, the doors opened and Violante was treated to a spectacular unobstructed view of the London skyline. Hartley was standing off to one side, like a master of ceremonies. It was a stunning effect, and Violante was impressed. Hartley waved at him to bring the car forward.

"I'm inside," Violante said for Reyna's benefit.

"I see the car," she said.

"Want me to wave?"

"Only if you need to be rescued."

Violante drove the car a few feet into the living room, put it into park, and switched off the engine.

Hartley approached the driver's side door and opened it. "Welcome to our humble home."

"There's nothing humble about it."

This was not at all how Violante expected an archaeologist to live. He thought it would be an old house filled with dusty books, ratty furniture, and lots of maritime crap. But this was more like the upscale apartment of a wealthy art collector. Once again, he'd misjudged Hartley. It was disturbing.

"I suppose you're right," Hartley said. "If you've seen the extraordinary riches that we have in our business, it's hard to satisfy or impress us with the usual trappings of success. So we have very expensive tastes."

It made sense to Violante after seeing the *Santa Isabel* treasure. He would soon have the same problem as the Hartleys. It would be difficult to impress him with any object once he possessed a solid gold table.

"Where's your lovely wife?"

"Somewhere safe, with her finger on the button, waiting to hear from me that everything has gone smoothly."

Just like Reyna is watching out for me, Violante thought.

• • •

"Wife?" Gooley asked into the radio. "What wife?"

The question was clearly meant for Kate, the Nicolas Fox expert. She picked up the radio and replied. "He's got to be referring to Serena Blake. She and Nick must have been running a con on Violante."

On the screen, she saw Violante walk to the rear of the Range Rover and open the back.

"They were swindling him?" Gooley said. "That changes everything."

"No, it doesn't," Kate said. "He's still here buying stolen goods."

"We don't know what he's buying. Or what he *thinks* he's buying. He could be an innocent sucker."

"He's not," Kate said. "Be patient."

Hartley whistled when he saw the silver cases. "So that's what twenty-five million dollars looks like."

"I hope you have a very big bathtub."

"We do." Hartley smiled and clapped Violante on the back as if they were old buddies. "Give me a hand unloading these."

"That won't be necessary," Violante said. "Keep the car."

"Wow. Are you sure?"

Violante didn't want to unpack the car. He wanted to get the treasure map and leave as soon as possible. "Consider it an apology for the misunderstanding in Marbella."

"Thank you," Hartley said, turning his back to Violante to

take another look at the Range Rover and the money. "That's very generous of you."

"Blue team," Gooley said on the radio, giving the go-ahead for the police chopper to launch from Lippitts Hill base in Loughton, thirteen miles northeast of central London.

"Affirmative," the pilot replied.

"Approach the nest from the south," Kate said into the radio. "Don't frighten the birds."

"What birds?" Gooley asked.

"The robin and the pigeon," Kate said. "The two in the bush."

"What are you talking about?"

"Fox will be spooked if he sees a police chopper heading his way. He's the robin, right? Or is he the pigeon?"

Kate was actually more concerned about spooking Violante.

"Roger that," Gooley said. "Blue team, stay wide, approach from the south."

Hartley lifted one of the suitcases out of the back of the SUV, took it to the coffee table, and opened it up. The euros were packed neatly inside. He took out a few stacks, set them on the tabletop, and selected a bill at random. He snapped it in his fingers, sniffed it, and held it up to the light.

"Are you an expert at authenticating cash?" Violante asked.

"Nope." Hartley took a magnifying glass from his pocket. "But I am a quick study. I've been reading up on the subject for a few weeks now."

While Hartley examined the bill, Violante went to one of the display cases and admired a gleaming jewel-encrusted golden goblet that had probably been salvaged from the bottom of the sea. He wondered how many wonderful treasures just like this that he'd find in the wreckage of the *Santa Isabel*.

"This appears genuine to me." Hartley dropped the bill on the table.

"So do we have a deal?"

Hartley walked over to Violante, took the goblet out of the display case, and handed it to him.

"Our treasure is all yours," Hartley said.

"That's it," Gooley said over the radio. "The exchange has been made. All units, move in!"

It was all in motion now, and Kate knew there would be no going back. Within a few seconds, police vehicles filled with officers in tactical assault gear would speed toward the Excelsior Tower from the north, across the Battersea and Albert bridges, and from the southeast from Battersea Park. Plus a police chopper would close in from the air.

In ten minutes it would all be over, and Demetrio Violante would be in custody for purchasing stolen art, and on the road to being revealed as Lester Menendez. And Nicolas Fox would be gone, to everyone's bewilderment and frustration.

That was the plan.

27

Nick popped the cork on the bottle of champagne while Violante examined the goblet.

We're counting down, Kate thought, watching Nick. Don't take too long to enjoy the champagne. Her attention turned to Violante when she saw him touch his ear and look over at the window. Holy crap, she thought, he's wearing an earbud.

"Are you sure?" Violante asked.

Nick stopped midpour with a glass in one hand and the bottle in the other. "Excuse me?"

"I wasn't talking to you, you idiot," Violante said to Nick.

"Who were you talking to?"

Violante ignored Nick and rushed to the window. His face, which was normally as smooth as custard, was contorted in rage.

He's wearing an undetectable earbud, Nick thought, and he's just been warned that the police are swarming in from the park and driving across the bridge. Kate had reached the same conclusion. The cop who was watching the monitors back at headquarters figured it out as well.

Violante gaped out the window at the police cars racing across the bridges and knew they were coming for him. Somehow, they'd discovered that he was Lester Menendez. Somehow, somewhere, he'd made a mistake or had been betrayed. How it happened didn't matter now, and neither did getting the treasure. The only thing that mattered was escaping from the police. If he could temporarily prevent them from locking down the building, and keep them too occupied to quickly regroup, he had a chance of getting away in the chaos.

Violante touched the earbud again. "Buy me some time."

"What's going on?" Nick asked.

"The police are surrounding the building. Is there another way out of here?"

"There's a maid's elevator in the utility corridor," Nick said. "You can take it to any floor you want or all the way down to the garage."

It's Reyna, Kate thought. Reyna was feeding information to Violante, and she had to be nearby. Close enough to have seen the police moving in. She had no way of knowing if Reyna was on land or on water, but Kate was guessing water. She hadn't seen Reyna in either of the vehicles that had transported

Violante and his money. And it would make sense to have a
backup river getaway.

Kate grabbed the binoculars, ran to the flybridge, and
scanned the water in front of her. *BANG*. A flare streaked across
the sky toward the Albert Bridge and landed with a blinding
flash of light on the roadway. There was a lot of thick red smoke
coming off the bridge, and instantly police band radio chatter
indicated that the bridge had taken a hit and traffic had come
to a standstill.

BANG, BANG, BANG. More flares. Two landed on the
Battersea Bridge, and the third landed on the Albert. There was
a lot more red smoke followed by the screech of tires and the
crashing of cars.

Kate had a fix on the source of the flares. They were coming
from a small powerboat that was sitting in the middle of the
Thames, in front of the Excelsior Tower, and midway between
the two bridges. She focused the binoculars on the boat and saw
Reyna alone at the helm.

Three Scotland Yard armored personnel carriers rolled up in
front of Excelsior Tower. Violante's four security guards instantly
threw their weapons onto the ground and put their hands over
their heads, hoping to avoid being shot by adrenaline-pumped
cops.

The rear doors of the personnel carriers flew open, and
dozens of officers spilled out, looking more like soldiers than
cops. They were in full tactical gear—Kevlar duty vests, ballistic

helmets, combat goggles, and flame-retardant balaclavas that almost entirely masked their faces.

A third of the officers took positions in front of the Excelsior, another third stormed the lobby and the garage, and the remaining third split up and moved toward the back of the building from both sides to begin drawing a perimeter.

Gooley stayed inside the command unit, which was now also parked in front of Excelsior Tower. He watched the monitors that showed him the feeds from Nick's flat, from the helmet-mounted cameras worn by his ground-team leaders, and from the CCTV cameras showing the chaos on the bridges.

He was determined not to let the traffic mess, and losing half his strike force, distract him from completing the mission. He'd still lock down the building. It was time to show Fox and Violante who was in charge.

The police chopper streaked overhead, and Gooley radioed the pilot with orders.

"Say hello and tell them they are under arrest."

Violante had watched Reyna dispatch the flares and knew the police officers advancing across the bridges were trapped behind the snarled traffic. Now all he had to do was create a disaster that would distract the officers arriving at the building. He got into the Range Rover, turned the ignition key, and released the parking brake. He shifted into drive and charged across the room, leaping out of the vehicle a beat before the front bumper touched the floor-to-ceiling window.

The police chopper came around the tower, went into a hover directly in front of the condo window, and the Range Rover smashed through the glass and shot out of the building. The chopper pilot peeled away, the Range Rover missed the helicopter by mere inches, and millions of euros were sucked out of the flat's broken window.

Gooley saw the astonishing sight from three angles. He saw the Range Rover burst out of the flat and fly head-on toward the chopper's camera. He saw the terrifying view from the ground leader's helmet camera as he glanced up at the sky to see the SUV dropping toward him. And the third view was from the surveillance feed.

The Range Rover plummeted to the ground and exploded on impact into an enormous fireball. The blast shattered hundreds of windows, raining down shards of glass, and euros fluttered in the air like butterflies.

"This is bad," Nick said to Violante. "These paintings need to be in a humidity-controlled environment, and you've broken the window."

"I don't give a rat's ass about the paintings," Violante said, getting to his feet. "How do I get out of here?"

Reyna saw the chopper swerve to avoid the Range Rover, and she took aim with a handheld rocket launcher. It wasn't every day that she got a chance to shoot down a helicopter. She was about to squeeze the trigger when she heard the roar of an engine off the stern. She turned and saw that a yacht was bearing down on her, a woman in a yellow police windbreaker at the wheel on the flybridge. She was pretty sure it was Kate Hartley. Wasn't that perfect. She always knew the woman wasn't what she seemed, but she hadn't guessed cop.

Reyna shouldered the rocket launcher and fired one off at the yacht. It streaked over the water and smashed through the front window of the main cabin, rocketed straight through the galley, and out the open door at the stern before hitting the water fifty yards away.

Kate ignored the grenade and kept the throttle fully open, plowing into the powerboat, ripping it apart, and sending Reyna into the river. The yacht didn't fare much better than the powerboat. It sustained a huge gash in the bow and immediately began to take on water. Kate ran to the dinghy at the back of the boat, untied it, and jumped in. She floated free of the yacht and was about to crank up the outboard when Reyna burst out of the black water, levered herself onto the dinghy, and lunged at Kate.

The two women rolled around in the bottom of the dinghy, scratching and clawing and punching. Reyna pulled a switch-blade out of her pants pocket, slashed at Kate, and Kate felt a searing flash of pain as the blade sliced into her.

Kate stuck her thumb into Reyna's eye, and flipped Reyna out of the boat. Reyna sank below the surface, and after a moment a blood slick appeared on the black swirling water. The blood slick dissipated, and Kate saw no more sign of Reyna.

The chopper swung away from the shoreline and hovered over the dinghy. Kate acknowledged the chopper with a nod of her head. She was bleeding from the stab wound in her side, and she suspected she had a broken bone in her hand. She had no clue if Reyna was alive or dead.

Nick led Violante across the apartment to a door he unlocked by typing a code into a wall-mounted keypad. The door opened and the two men stepped into a narrow windowless service corridor that contained the maid's entrance to the next condo, the stairwell, and the elevator.

"That's your way out," Nick said, gesturing to the elevator, "unless you want to take the stairs."

Violante pressed the elevator call button.

"If you help the police, or sell the treasure to anyone else, I will behead you," Violante said to Nick.

"You haven't escaped yet."

"I will," Violante said. "I have nine lives, and I have used up only two of them."

Nick punched Violante with a right hook that dropped him to the floor. Violante's head bounced off the concrete, his eyes went blank, and he was out cold.

Nick felt for a pulse, and found that it was still strong. He returned to the condo, grabbed a pen from the desk in the office, and used it to write MENENDEZ across Violante's forehead.

Nick walked down the corridor, opened the servant's entrance to the unsold unit next door, and stepped inside. A police officer's full tactical suit and weapons were laid out on a drafting table.

28

Kate sat on the edge of the bed in the emergency room at Chelsea and Westminster Hospital. She had two fingers taped together on her right hand and fourteen stitches in her side just under her rib cage. The stab wound had been painful and bloody but fortunately not deep enough to do bad damage.

The curtain surrounding the bed was pulled aside, and Gooley stepped in. He was no longer in tactical gear but back in his leather and sheepskin coat. He handed Kate a bag of Krispy Kremes.

"At least we don't have to go to the bother of auctioning off that yacht," Gooley said, "being that it's at the bottom of the Thames." He rocked back on his heels. "You ever drive a boat before?"

"I spotted Violante's bodyguard, Reyna Socorro, in the

powerboat. She was positioned between the two bridges, shooting off the flares. Sorry about the yacht, but it was my only weapon."

"Not your only weapon," Gooley said. "We pulled Reyna out of the Thames with her eye gouged out and a broken nose."

"Is she okay?"

"She was full of river water," Gooley said.

"What about Violante and Fox?"

"We got Violante. He was found knocked out in a stairwell, and he had 'Menendez' written across his forehead. It looked like he'd been punched in the face. Fox got away."

"He usually does."

"We had the building surrounded. It was like he sprouted wings and flew out the open window."

Not wings, Kate thought. Nick had made himself invisible by wearing the same tactical outfit as the police who were storming the building. He probably walked right past Gooley.

"At a press conference tomorrow, Scotland Yard will flog this as a successful joint operation with U.S. law enforcement agencies," Gooley said. "The press will be told it resulted in the apprehension of a highly dangerous international felon. We'll also hint that a stunning revelation about the true identity of that felon is forthcoming, pending further investigation. Privately, the Yard is getting a slagging from Downing Street for a monumental cock-up that turned a half-kilometer stretch of the Thames into a war zone."

"Have you heard from Hollywood yet?"

"No, but I told dispatch to put Russell Crowe straight through to me when he calls." Gooley offered Kate his hand. "What you did on the Thames today took guts. You're one hell of a copper."

"So are you."

"Cheers, then." He nodded his thanks and walked out.

Kate looked into the donut bag, and a doctor in surgical scrubs, mask, and cap came in.

"We're ready to remove your spleen," he announced in a British accent that sounded remarkably like Roger Moore's.

"Can I eat my donuts first?" Kate asked.

"I wouldn't if I were you. You're already pushing the limits on those jeans you're wearing."

"I know it's you," Kate said to Nick. "That's the worst British accent ever. What are you doing here?"

"I was hoping you'd show me your stitches."

"I'm not showing you *anything*."

"I took a big risk coming here to visit you. You could at least show me *something*."

Kate showed him the two fingers that were taped together, one of which was her middle finger.

"Nice," Nick said. "Just what I'd expect from the woman who intentionally rammed a yacht into a powerboat."

"I hear someone punched Violante in the face."

"Only because I didn't have a yacht handy to plow into him. He had it coming."

"That and more," Kate said. "We've destroyed him."

"Yeah, this assignment is done, but I have a loose end to tie up."

"Serena?"

"I need to give her the good news."

"And break her out of prison?"

"You don't really want to know, do you?"

"No." Kate grimaced. "Yes."

"Which is it?"

"It's *yes,* and I'm going with you."

"What about the stitches?"

"There are only fourteen of them. Let's not overdramatize this."

"I can't take you into the prison with me, but I'll let you drive the getaway car," Fox said.

"Deal."

This wasn't a gig assigned by Jessup, but Kate had been given the responsibility of babysitting Nick and she was going to do it. She couldn't talk him out of springing Serena, but she could hang in there and try to minimize the damage.

La Maison d'arrêt d'Orléans was built in 1896 on the outskirts of the city to hold seventy-five men and a dozen women. Now the prison was surrounded by apartment buildings, and it held more than two hundred men and women awaiting trial. One of those women was Serena Blake.

Security at the prison was notoriously lax, and the prison had the distinction of being the noisiest one in the country, at least on the outside. People gathered day and night on the sidewalks, and on the rooftops and decks of nearby apartment buildings, to communicate with the prisoners by yelling back and forth, infuriating local residents who couldn't get any peace. These same people routinely threw cellphones, cigarettes, knives, sandwiches, drugs, and other items over the low stone and concrete walls to prisoners on the other side.

Nick Fox didn't choose this method to communicate with Serena Blake. Fox masqueraded as her attorney, Jean-Luc Picard. He arrived at the prison in an ancient black Mercedes, accompanied by Kate and Boyd Capwell. Boyd wore a weather-beaten leather coat with wide sheepskin-lined lapels that looked as if it might have been stolen from a homeless man who'd used it as bedding.

Kate parked in the small lot in front of the prison, the buildings within hidden from street-level view behind the gray wall that encircled the property. This was the prison's only entrance, a rectangular opening as wide as a four-car garage, with a thick iron-barred gate and, to one side, a tiny guardhouse. Kate had on a knit cap with her hair tucked up inside. She was wearing a bulky jacket with the collar turned up, and Nick had transformed her face with makeup and prosthetic padding so that she would be unrecognizable to Serena.

Nick had told Boyd that they were helping to free a woman who'd been framed for a crime. "Are you ready?" Nick asked him. "Everything rides on you being convincing."

"This is nothing. I played Inspector Javert in the animated version of *Les Misérables.*"

"The one with the singing mice?"

"I imbued a mouse with moral authority and an all-consuming obsession while carrying a tune in a squeaky French accent. Next time, give me a real challenge."

"There was no danger involved in that. Now you're impersonating a real police officer and walking into a prison full of armed guards."

"They don't scare me," Boyd said. "I've faced drama critics. They can be inhuman."

Nick nodded, satisfied. "Then let's do it."

Kate stayed with the car, and Nick and Boyd got out and walked to the guardhouse. They could hear people on the street yelling at the prisoners inside and the muffled voices of the prisoners yelling back from the open windows of their cells.

Nick smiled at the guard and greeted him in French.

"Look at you. Who is the real prisoner here?" Nick asked the guard. "You or the men inside?"

"I ask myself the same question every day. At least they have room to turn around in their cells," the guard said.

"Ah, but do they go home to the love of a good woman every night?"

"You obviously haven't met my wife," the guard said and roared with laughter.

"Oh, for God's sake!" Boyd said, speaking in English with a thick Manchester accent. "I'm Detective Chief Inspector Dennis

Gooley, London Metropolitan Police. Can we speed this up? I've got a plane to catch, and I need to get my prisoner."

Nick sighed and spoke again in French to the guard. "The British have no appreciation for pleasant conversation. And I am going to be stuck beside him on a plane."

"I'd rather be in this shack," the guard said.

The guard took Boyd's ID and handed Nick a clipboard. "Have him sign this form. The assistant warden will meet you in front of the women's cell block with your client."

Boyd signed the form, the guard pressed a button, the gate opened, and Nick and Boyd stepped inside the prison grounds.

The prison block was three stories tall, but could have passed for a 1950s-era high school or library, if not for the bars in front of the windows. They were met outside the door by a timid, thin little man with pale skin who wore a rumpled black suit and looked more like an undertaker than a bureaucrat. He carried a sheaf of papers under his arm.

"Inspector Gooley, I am Maksud Attard, assistant warden," Attard said in English. "We received the paperwork this morning from our Ministry of Justice approving the extradition request by the British authorities. I must say it's a most unusual situation."

"Everything my client was alleged to have stolen has been recovered," Nick said. "The French authorities have nothing to gain by keeping her."

"Except justice," Attard said. "They caught her red-handed."

"It's a plea bargain," Boyd said. "She's agreed to help us catch the thief who was her accomplice in exchange for a lighter sentence to be served entirely in the UK."

Attard shook his head. "You must be a remarkable lawyer, Monsieur Picard, to have managed that deal."

Nick agreed. *"C'est vrai."*

Boyd made a derisive sound. "Serena Blake is a small fish compared to her pal Nick Fox. Every law enforcement agency involved jumped at the chance to trade her for Fox. And Serena would sell out her own mum to avoid a Turkish prison. A monkey could've made this deal."

The door to the cell block opened and Serena Blake was brought out by two guards.

Boyd stepped up to her, placed a handcuff on her right wrist, closed it tight, and then closed the other cuff on his left wrist. "You're nicked, doll."

Serena looked at Boyd like he smelled bad. And, in fact, he didn't smell all that wonderful in the ratty coat.

Attard held some papers and a pen out to Boyd. "Sign these and she's in your custody."

Boyd signed the papers. One copy was given to him, another to Nick, and Attard kept the third. Nick, Boyd, and Serena walked out the gate and took their time getting to the Mercedes. Kate was behind the wheel, Boyd and Serena slid into the backseat, and Nick took the passenger seat beside Kate. Kate backed out of the parking space and drove down Boulevard Guy-Marie Riobé, passing a taxi heading in the opposite direction. The taxi's passenger was a man wearing a leather-and-sheepskin coat that looked exactly like the one Boyd was wearing.

Kate pulled to the side of the road and parked behind a gray panel van. Everyone got out of the Mercedes, piled into the van, and Kate drove off.

"That went as smooth as silk," Boyd said. "I was excellent."

"You were a credit to the coat," Nick told him.

"My prison cell smelled better than this coat," Serena said. "Could we lose the coat and the cuffs?"

Boyd unlocked the cuffs, took the coat off, and Serena threw the coat out the window.

29

Kate dropped Serena off at the train station, and Serena headed for parts unknown. Boyd was dropped off on the right bank of the Seine, where he was meeting an actor friend. And Kate and Nick continued on to the airport, where they would board separate planes back to the United States.

Kate parked the van, stripped off her fake face, and left the bulky jacket and cap on the backseat.

"Do you think Serena recognized me?" she asked Nick.

"No," he answered. "And if she did, I don't think she'll ever say anything to anybody. I'm sure she's grateful to have this end."

"I'm happy to have this operation behind me," Kate said when they arrived at the terminal. "I'm still not sure we did the right thing."

"All's well that ends well," Nick said. "All of the stolen art has been returned. Menendez will never see the light of day. And Boyd gets to have a couple days in Paris. It's all good."

Kate's cellphone buzzed, and she flinched when she saw the caller ID. It was her boss, Carl Jessup.

"I just received a text message that less than an hour ago Serena Blake escaped from prison," Jessup said. "Did you have anything to do with it?"

"Of course not," Kate said. "That would be a crime."

"I'm glad to hear you still know where to draw the line."

"How did the escape go down?" Kate asked.

"Gooley arranged to have Serena extradited to England, but when he got to the prison in Orléans to pick her up, he discovered that she'd already been released to someone masquerading as him."

"Very clever."

"Clever enough to be arranged by Nick Fox."

"Yes, sir."

"We can't be involved in breaking criminals out of prison," Jessup said.

Kate made crackling sounds into the phone. "You're breaking up," she said. "Can't hear you." And she disconnected.

Nick raised his eyebrows in question.

"Jessup heard about Serena's escape," Kate said.

"Good news travels fast."

"He didn't think it was good news."

"Good news is relative." Nick glanced at his watch. "You need to check in. My plane doesn't leave for a while, so I'm going to the lounge."

"Try to stay out of trouble," Kate said.

Nick grabbed her, pulled her close against him, and kissed her. There was some tongue involved and a little discreet groping.

"Zoinks!" she said when he released her.

"It gets even better," he said. "I've got something you can wrap your hand around and really enjoy."

And he slipped a giant-sized Toblerone bar into the pocket of her sweatshirt.

ABOUT THE AUTHORS

JANET EVANOVICH is the #1 *New York Times* bestselling author of the Stephanie Plum series, the Fox and O'Hare series with co-author Lee Goldberg, the Lizzy and Diesel series, twelve romance novels, the Alexandra Barnaby novels and Troublemaker graphic novel, and *How I Write: Secrets of a Bestselling Author.*

www.evanovich.com
Facebook.com/JanetEvanovich
@JanetEvanovich

LEE GOLDBERG is a screenwriter, TV producer, and the author of several books, including *King City, The Walk,* and the bestselling Monk series of mysteries. He has earned two Edgar Award nominations and was the 2012 recipient of the Poirot Award from Malice Domestic.

www.leegoldberg.com
Facebook.com/AuthorLeeGoldberg
@LeeGoldberg

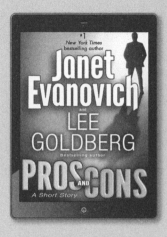
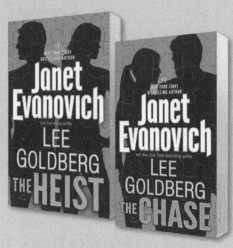
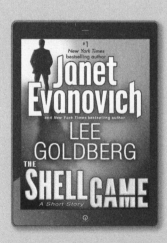
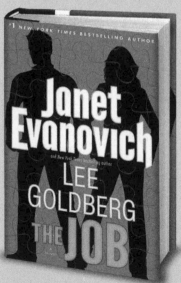

THE WAIT IS OVER.
Lizzy and Diesel are
BACK!

WICKED CHARMS

ON SALE 3.10.15

AND DON'T MISS

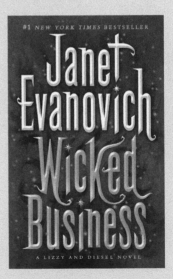